5/12

You Will Call Me

DROG

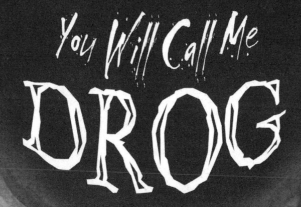

You Will Call Me DROG

SUE COWING

CAROLRHODA BOOKS

MINNEAPOLIS

Carolrhoda Books
A division of Lerner Publishing Group, Inc.
241 First Avenue North
Minneapolis, MN 55401 U.S.A.

Website address: www.lernerbooks.com

Cover and interior photographs © Klotz/Dreamstime.com (puppet); © Photodisc/
Getty Images (curtain); © iStockphoto.com/JazzIRT (hand).

Main body text set in Origami Std 12/16.
Typeface provided by Monotype Typography.

Library of Congress Cataloging-in-Publication Data

Cowing, Sue, 1938–
        You will call me Drog / by Sue Cowing.
            p.   cm.
        Summary: Unless eleven-year-old Parker can find a way to remove the
    sinister puppet that refuses to leave his hand, he will wind up in military
    school or worse but first he must stand up for himself to his best friend, Wren;
    his mother; and his nearly absent father.
        ISBN: 978-0-7613-6076-6 (trade hard cover : alk. paper)
        [1. Puppets—Fiction. 2. Supernatural—Fiction. 3. Self-confidence—Fiction.
    4. Interpersonal relations—Fiction. 5. Divorce—Fiction. 6. Aikido—Fiction.
    7. Illinois—Fiction.] I. Title.
    PZ7.C8366You 2011
    [Fic]—dc22

                                                            2010050891

Manufactured in the United States of America
1 – SB – 7/15/11

For Ced and
Jim Cowing

—S.C.

PART I

The Opponent

chapter one

Wren and I spent Sunday at Ferrisburg Salvage and Iron, rummaging through piles of car doors and broken chairs for treasures to load onto our bikes. We had just promised ourselves that next time we'd bring a wagon for the iron birdcage and were about to go home to get warm when Wren pointed at something sticking out of the trash can.

"Look, Parker. A doll."

I let go of my bike and pulled the thing out by the head. It felt light. Just a head, arms, and a hollow shirt. "It's a hand puppet," I said.

It smelled like a damp basement. Its painted eyes stared right at me.

Wren looked closer at it and a shudder went through her. "Creepy," she said. "Let's leave it."

It *was* weird-looking. Bald green head, crackly skin, and

a shirt made out of old-time couch material. But I didn't want to just throw it back.

"We could repaint it or something," I said.

Wren gripped her handlebars and kicked up her kickstand. "You can if you want, Parker. Just put it away, will you?"

Why was she being so bossy? About an old puppet? I stuck it in my backpack.

If I'd listened to Wren that day, maybe I'd have just gone on being the same old pretty happy, pretty ordinary kid.

We pedaled down Main Street, which was so empty on Sunday afternoon that a couple of pigeons fought over something in the middle of the street, and we could see all the way down to the square. Two men were carrying a ladder and paint cans into the building with papered-up windows where the furniture store used to be. The tall one had straight black hair and looked Asian.

Suddenly the shorter man turned to say something, knocking into the tall one with the ladder. He fell forward and a paint can flew out of his hand, but he did a kind of somersault and came up under the can, catching it before it could hit the ground. The two men laughed and bowed to each other.

What was that all about? Any other time, we would have gone down to see, but Wren's mom was having people over for dinner, and she had to get home.

We turned at the Swanson Feed Store, got off our bikes and bumped them across the railroad tracks. Then we headed down Prairie Street to my house, because I had more space for stuff. A whole room, in fact, that used to be my dad's home office. Mom let me keep anything in there that didn't smell bad or explode.

Wren rode on home while I brought in our day's haul and dumped everything out on the floor: stroller wheels, some smooth blocks of pinewood, a dented trumpet. If I half-closed my eyes and looked at them, they might tell me what they wanted to be.

But I couldn't stop thinking about the puppet. What if I invented a huge wind-up toy with the puppet playing the trumpet? I hauled my backpack up to my room to make some sketches.

Sweeping the Legos off my desk, I got out a pencil and paper and pulled the puppet out of my pack. I couldn't seem to get it to go on, so I tried it on my left hand. Perfect fit. Funny, I never thought there were left- and right-hand puppets.

I cleaned the dirt off it with my T-shirt. The minute I wiped its face, it said, "You will call me Drog."

Whoa. I whipped my head around. Nobody else in the room.

"Zounds, Boy!" the voice said. "You actually live in this hovel?"

That had to be coming from the puppet.

"Hov— hovel?" I guess he meant the unmade bed and the towels on the floor. I loved my room, actually. The wall of drawers with handles I could climb to the ledge on top to read or draw. The old iron radiator that clanged on cold mornings. The window that opened out into the crabapple tree. With the leaves gone for the winter, I could see through the backyards all the way to Wren's house.

I swallowed and shook my head to clear it. Was this puppet really talking? Was I really answering? Weird.

"To think that I once enjoyed a whole wing of my own in the emir's palace," Drog said, "and dined with him on ice cream sprinkled with gold dust."

Huh? "What's . . . a emir?"

Drog sighed. "What is an emir? An emir, dear boy, is the ruler of a *civilized* country in the Middle East. Like Oh Man. Or Cat-man Doo."

"Like a president?"

"Certainly not! A president has to worry about what other people think. A *ruler*, I say! A prince! A man of power and wealth!"

I checked him over to see what was making him talk, but I couldn't find a switch or button or anything. Must be inside somewhere, but then wouldn't I feel it?

Little thrills shot through me. *Wait'll I tell Wren*, I thought to myself. If we figured this talking puppet out, maybe we could make one.

I pulled him off to have a look inside. I mean, I tried to. I tugged on his head and hands, but nothing happened.

"You waste your time," he said.

I pulled some more.

Drog laughed. "Give it up, Boy. Wherever you go, there go I."

Suddenly I really wanted him off. I stuck my thumb inside and pulled, but he squeezed tight on my hand and wouldn't let me budge him. I tugged again, harder. He squeezed again.

"Ah, you see?" he said.

I pulled on him again.

He squeezed.

I yanked.

He squeezed.

This is not happening. It can't be.

"Cut it out! Let go!"

Mom called up the stairs. "Parker? Is Wren up there with you?"

My mouth opened.

"Parker?"

"No, Mom." I croaked.

"Well, come on down. Supper's ready."

"*Now* what?" I moaned. "I can't—"

"Not a problem. Put me in your pocket."

"Oh. Yeah."

Once he was out of sight and quiet, I calmed down some.

I ate supper with one hand, pretending I was keeping my other hand in my lap like you're supposed to. Between bites I focused on the two patches in the kitchen floor so Mom wouldn't look at me and ask if something was wrong.

I made those patches from some linoleum scraps Wren's dad said I could keep. One patch I cut into the shape of a squirrel and the other one into an acorn. Mom couldn't get over the great job I did, and the next time Dad came to pick me up for the weekend, she made him come into the kitchen and see.

Dad.

Mom shook my arm. "Hello? Parker? You're daydream- . ing. Aren't you hungry?"

I forked some macaroni into my mouth with my right hand, but it turned to gravel going down.

After supper, Mom curled up on the living room couch to read her latest mystery, so I shut the door and grabbed the phone.

"Wren! You'll never believe what's happening!"

"What?!" I could hear adults laughing and talking in the background.

"You know that puppet I found at the junkyard?

"Uh . . . *you* found?"

"Well, his name is Drog."

"Frog?"

"No, Drog. And guess what, he talks all by himself, and I can't—"

"It talks? That's incredible!"

"I know. His face stays the same and his mouth doesn't move, but he talks, and I can't—"

"Wow! Wouldn't it be great if we could make our own?"

"That's what I thought, but—"

"Hmmmm. Must have a memory chip or something. You checked inside?"

"No, I . . . I haven't told you the weirdest part. Could you just come over?"

chapter two

I slipped out onto the front porch to wait for her and shivered.

"Don't expect me to speak a word to that creature," Drog said. "Imagine! Calling Drog a doll!"

A freight train wailed in the distance. Probably headed for Chicago. Normally, I liked that sound, but right then it felt like a far-off scream. I stared at the nightmare on my hand and wanted to scream myself.

Hurry, Wren!

Finally she came around the corner, hopscotched up the walk, and flopped down on the porch steps.

"Show me!" she said, like this was going to be exciting.

I sank down next to her and held up my Drog hand.

Silence.

"Drog, tell Wren about the emir. About his gold-dust ice cream."

I waited. Wren waited. Those painted eyes gazed into space.

"I thought you said it talks, Parker. Here, let me try it."

"Um, that's the trouble, Wren. I . . . can't get him off."

"Oh, come on," she said and pulled on his head.

Drog stuck to me like cement.

"Hey, why won't you let me try?"

"Wren, listen. I can't get him off. And he really does talk. It's just—I guess he only talks to certain people."

Her eyebrows scrunched together. "Stop it, will you? This isn't funny."

"Stop what?"

"Whatever it is you're doing. Or at least let me in on it."

"I can't, Wren. That's what I keep trying to tell you."

"Parker. This puppet does not talk."

"Yes he *does*, you have to believe me! But he told me . . . he wouldn't talk to you."

"Oh."

She sat back and picked at some loose paint on the porch step.

"Is that why you asked me over? To tell me you're having private conversations with this puppet?"

"No, Wren, I—"

"I knew we should have left it at the junkyard. Now it's got you making up stories and being . . . a pig."

Her eyes shut halfway, and she studied me, waiting. For what?

Then she hauled herself up, zipped her jacket, and jammed her hands in the pockets, "Well you can talk to *your* puppet all you want. I'm going back home now."

"Wren, wait. You don't understand. I need—"

She turned back toward me. "You need to take that *Drog* back where you got it."

Then she was gone.

Please, Wren. Don't leave me alone with this. You can't!

But wishing hard into the space she'd left behind didn't bring her back.

"Now look what you did!" I said to Drog.

"What?" he crooned. "I did you a favor."

Mom opened the front door. "Did I hear Wren? Sounded like arguing out here."

"Yeah, well, she doesn't think much of this puppet I found."

"Oh, is that all?"

I shook my head. "He doesn't think much of her, either."

She smiled, like I was making a joke.

"Gotta do my homework," I mumbled and ducked inside.

I did have days of assignments to do, mostly math, but there was no way I could start any of it. I holed up in my room and tried to watch TV with the sound off. All I could see, though, was a hideous talking puppet where my hand ought to be. And no Wren. She wasn't just any friend. How could she leave me with this?

When she moved to town the summer before third grade, Wren Rivera was like no kid I'd ever known. Instead of growing up in Ferrisburg with us, she'd lived in a kind of rough neighborhood near Chicago. She was half Mexican and part German and part something else I forget, and she had a father who worked out of his garage and drank hot chocolate instead of coffee and made tacos stuffed with mashed potatoes and chili peppers for their Sunday breakfast. No one else we knew called their father Papa.

Wren wore her hair in one long braid and carried an egg-shaped stone in her pocket that she said was probably an agate. Everybody was curious about her, but nobody thought about being her friend.

Except me. One Saturday she was read-walking a book on Illinois rocks and minerals down the aisle at the library and ran right into me. We ended up at her house that day, looking over the rocks in her collection—flints, quartzes, a geode—even a fossil worm. None of them came from a rock shop. She found them all herself and looked them up.

Right then I knew we were more alike than any other two kids in town. We both really go after something we're interested in until we've done everything we can about it. We get each other into it, too. Without me, Wren would never have gone poking around in the junkyard. Without her, I might never have thought about what was inside of rocks.

She told me she found her pocket stone in a streambed on the way to Ferrisburg. A couple of mineral stains and markings on it that I barely noticed made her think it was an agate. She hoped so, because it would be her first. I asked her why she didn't just break it open and see if it was, but she said, "Right now I just want to believe it is." She wished it could be a fire agate or a crazy lace, but those you could only find in Mexico or the Southwest, she said.

She brought out a whole book just on agates and showed me the pictures. The fire agates glowed like opals, and the crazy-lace patterns looked like rings and veins of colored parsley or holly leaves.

There were lots of other cool ones too. Most had bands of color coming out from the center—like wavy growth rings or lava flows or raccoon eyes. The colors might be milky blues and grays or bright orange and red and moss green. And they all had formed inside totally ordinary-looking rocks.

I wasn't in a hurry for Wren to crack open her stone, either. As long as she didn't, almost any one of those patterns or colors in the book could be inside—or something else completely. It was more fun to think about that way.

I might not even have gotten started with carpentry if it wasn't for Wren. That first day, she took me out to her dad's shop in the garage, where he was working on this amazing project, a whole miniature house for her, open on one side, with everything made of wood—a winding staircase, inlaid floors, and cabinets with little drawers that pulled out. Wren was helping him sand and glue and decide what went where. To me that garage full of sawdust and oiled tools was a magic shop, and Mr. Rivera was the magician who would teach me secrets.

Wren and I spent what was left of that summer hanging out in her dad's shop and building a tree house in the crabapple tree at my house. One day, when we were up in the tree daring each other to eat the sour fruit, Wren told me a secret.

"I'm learning Spanish," she said. "Online. Only don't tell Papa."

"Okay. But why not?"

"He wants me to wait until I can take it in high school and learn it right. He won't even speak it to me, except for a few words. He says his Spanish isn't good."

"But you want to start now."

She nodded. "I can't help it. Spanish is fun. It makes everything sound like you're singing. *La violeta, las montanas, la jirafa. Muy delicioso, no?*"

I laughed and answered "*Si*," one of the only Spanish words I knew. I could hear what she meant, but some of that singing had to be from the way she said the words.

"Papa says if I do well in Spanish class, he'll take me on a trip to South America or even Spain so I can practice."

"You'll do it. Wren. I bet you do well in everything." *Not like me.*

Her face got red. And then I told her a secret of mine.

"After Mom and Dad got divorced," I said, "I used to climb up here every day, even if it was raining. That way I could cry all I wanted and only the wind would hear me."

I couldn't help crying again right then, just thinking about it. Wren listened and rolled her pocket stone against her knee for a while, then she scrambled down and ran home. In a few minutes she came back with one half of her prize geode and put it in my hand.

"Keep it, amigo," she said.

The thing was dull and rough like a ball of concrete on the outside, but inside was a small cave full of icy pink crystals pointing toward the center. She said that the day she cracked that geode open, the field trip leader told her, "You are the first one to see this in a hundred million years." And half of it was mine.

That was Wren. We might get mad at each other sometimes, but Wren stood by me. Even when Dad got married again and I said some stupid things for a while. How could she give up on me now—over a stuck-up puppet?

She couldn't. By morning she'd be back on my side, and between the two of us we'd figure out what to do. Meanwhile, I was on my own.

"Bedtime, Drog," I said, trying hard to sound matter-of-fact. It was only eight-thirty. "I can't sleep with you on, so—"

I yanked on him again, but he held tight. Does he even sleep? I wondered. I flicked off the light and sank down on my bed. If he did, maybe he'd come loose and I could get him off me.

"Now, then," Drog said. "I shall tell you a bedtime story."

"A bedtime story? I'm not a little kid."

"Excellent. Because this isn't a little kid's story. It's about Farina, the emir's favorite dancing girl. Raven hair down to her toes, skin like silk, bones like water, and spangles where she jangled, if you know what I mean. Whew! My lights flicker just thinking about her."

I kicked my shoes across the room. "Drog, I—"

"One day the emir clapped his hands to summon her, but she didn't appear. Found her in the linen closet, but she would not come out."

"Why not?"

Drog ignored me.

"'Alas, I can no longer dance for you,' she said.

"No one refuses a summons from the emir, you understand. But he had a weakness for her, so he said, 'Oh please, you shall have apricots and pomegranates, pendants of lapis lazuli—'"

It was creepy how the puppet switched voices like that.

"Farina lifted her skirt to show him her once-delicate feet. They were now bright orange and webbed like a duck's."

"How come?" I asked.

"Sorcery, most probably. One of the emir's jealous wives must have—"

He nodded off right in the middle of his own sentence. He even started to snore. But as soon as I tried pulling him off, he contracted on my hand.

I let him get back to snoring. Then I pretended I just accidentally rubbed him against the bed frame in my sleep. He tightened again.

No more accidentally. I scraped him against the bed and the desk. I yanked on his head, his hands, his shirt. My heart boomed, *ga-whomp, ga-whomp*. Could an eleven-year-old have a heart attack?

I reached back to smash him against the wall, but he squeezed my hand so hard I thought my fingers would pop.

"My, my, my," he said. "You don't understand, do you?"

"No! I don't understand!"

"Very simple," he said, easing up. "You stop trying to get me off, I stop squeezing."

"Parker?" Mom called from her room. "Anything wrong?"

"Ah," Drog whispered, "are we going to cry for Mama?"

I had to answer her. "No, Mom. It's—I had a nightmare."

She came to the door. "Want to tell me about it?"

I shoved Drog under my pillow. "No, that's okay. I'm all right." I couldn't believe I said that.

"Sure? You don't sound all right."

I nodded, so I wouldn't have to speak.

"Well, good night, then. Take it easy, honey."

I waved with my free hand.

She leaned against the doorjamb a minute, then left. I took Drog out again.

"That's more like it," he said. "This is just between you and me."

"What is?" I said, clenching my teeth to stop their chatter-racketing. "Why are you doing this?"

"Why? Drog doesn't need a reason."

"But why me, Drog? Haven't I been a pretty good kid?"

"I have no idea. Why would you want to be a good kid?"

Some words raced around way in the back of my mind, and then I remembered what they were: *If thy right hand offend thee, cut it off.* That's from the Bible, I think. It gave me an idea.

My problem was with my left hand, not my right, and I sure didn't want to cut either one off. Just Drog. I waited for him to go back to sleep. Waited a few extra minutes to be sure. Then I kept my left arm as still as I could so I wouldn't wake him up while I felt all around on my desk with my right hand—pencils, marker, bike key, then the cool metal of the scissors.

Drog woke right up. "Do you really think your left hand doesn't know what your right hand is doing?"

I held on to the scissors and opened them.

"I wouldn't, if I were you," he said.

My hand stopped in midair. His voice sounded so icy. So superior.

"Well, you're— you're not me," I said.

"Oh? I am now, ha-ha! Anyway, as I was telling you, at the sight of those ugly duck feet the emir went into a rage. . . ."

I dropped the scissors onto the desk and fell back on the pillow.

What if what Drog said was true? What if he was becoming a part of me, some kind of jabbering mutant growth? I had to get out of this. *Think, think.*

My sheet twisted up and my eyeballs dried out—and then I heard the sudden quiet and let out my breath. Drog was asleep.

For once, I was glad Dad wasn't around to know what was going on. What would he do if this happened to him?

Dumb question. Nothing like this would ever happen to him, and not just because he wouldn't go poking around in the junkyard in the first place. Dad's an engineer. Everything in his world has to follow what he calls the rules of logic. It just does. He wouldn't have *let* anything this weird happen to him. So it must be my fault. But how?

Take it easy, I told myself. Just get through till tomorrow, and then figure something out.

I have my own sort of a bedtime story. I close my eyes and picture my hands moving blocks of wood around, not just rectangles and triangles, but bananas and curvy worms and zigzag shapes—whatever I think of. The more I fool with them, the more they go together to make fantastic patterns or objects, and then my hands get all warm and happy and I fall asleep. Works every time.

But that night I kept waking up and remembering all over again—*a puppet's got my hand.*

chapter three

I hid Drog in my pocket through breakfast, then struggled into my jacket and ran out to the corner to meet Wren, but she must have gone some other way to school.

I found her on the playground, though. She frowned when she saw me, but then she came over. "Hey Parker, you okay?" she said. "You look awful."

I pulled Drog a little way out of my pocket, then stuffed him back in. "Didn't sleep too much," I said.

"Oh. The puppet," she said. Her voice sounded flat. "How come you brought it to school?"

"Wren, I can't get him off. I told you."

Her eyes hunted mine. "I hope you're not going to try to tell everybody it talks," she said.

"No way! I'm going to keep him in my pocket the whole day so he won't talk at all. Do you think you could . . . ?"

Wren glanced around us and lowered her voice. "Please tell me what's going on, Parker. I'm getting kind of scared about you."

Scared? Scared was worse than mad. "I *am* telling you. Are you deaf or something?" Right away part of me wished I hadn't said that, but part of me was glad.

She stepped back, shocked.

"Oh come on, Wren, I didn't—"

"I guess maybe you're right. Maybe I am deaf. Because I don't hear any puppets talking."

We climbed the stairs to Mrs. Belcher's room. Together, but not together.

"Sorry," I said, "I shouldn't have said that about being deaf. I really need you to help me. Just . . . don't tell anybody about Drog, okay?"

"Who, me?"

———

"Hey, Parker," Gordy called out when I walked in, "I signed us out a basketball for recess so we can play horse."

"Um. Not today."

"How come? You sick or something?"

"Something."

He looked at me funny, then went to ask somebody else.

School turned out to be pretty hard one-handed. Without my left hand to hold the paper still, my handwriting got scribblier than ever. It was even harder to open a book and turn the pages.

After lunch Wren passed me a note:

I don't understand why you're making up all this puppet stuff. Why can't you just tell me? I thought you were my friend.

Wren

Unfair! I was about to write back and say, *If you're such a good friend, why don't you believe me?* But I didn't get the chance. Because while I was reading Wren's note, I forgot to keep Drog in my pocket.

Mrs. Belcher noticed. "Parker, what's that you have on your hand?"

It sounded too dumb to say "a puppet," so I just held Drog up.

Twenty-six faces swung around to look.

"Good afternoon, kiddies," Drog said.

I knew right then my life was over.

The kids grinned, all except Wren. Gordy, my recess buddy, called across the room, "Awright, *Parker!*" So everybody thought it was me talking.

"Put that away until after school, please," Mrs. Belcher said.

I shoved Drog back in my pocket.

"No, Parker, I mean away. Put it in your desk."

I stuck my whole Drog hand into my desk.

The kids turned clear around in their seats to watch the show.

"Parker, whatever you have there, come up and give it to me. Now."

I walked up to Mrs. Belcher's desk feeling sweaty stare-holes all over my back and said, practically in a whisper, "I can't."

"Excuse me?"

I went through the motions of trying to pull Drog off, then shrugged.

"Nice fit, don't you think?" Drog said.

I spun around toward Wren. "Did you hear that?"

She sighed. "That was you."

"Parker, I'm losing my patience." That was Mrs. Belcher— code for cease and desist.

"I'm sorry. I mean, it's not me, it's him, he keeps—"

"I think I'm going to let you explain it to Mr. Fairweather," she said.

Wren shook her head as I walked out.

<hr />

The counselor's office smelled like old cardboard boxes. Mr. Fairweather studied Mrs. Belcher's note.

"Parker Lockwood, hmm? When's the last time you were in to see me, Parker?

"I've never been to see you, Mr. Fairweather."

The most trouble I'd ever been in at school was in fifth grade, when some kids asked me to draw cool fake tattoos on them and I used permanent markers. The teacher handled that himself though and didn't turn me in.

Mr. Fairweather leaned back in his chair. "Well now, how does it happen that you keep your nose clean for six years, and today you get sent to me? A sudden interest in spitballs?"

"No."

"Fighting?"

"No."

"Talking back?"

"No."

"Hormones?"

"Hormones?"

"Never mind. Just tell me what happened."

I showed him Drog, and he sat straight up and wrote things down. I hated to tell him Drog talked, but how else was I going to explain?

"Anything special bothering you at the moment?" he asked me.

Besides not being able to get a nasty puppet off my hand? I shook my head.

"Hmmmm," Mr. Fairweather said, and leaned back in his chair again. "I think it would be a good idea for you to leave that puppet at home tomorrow."

I already had that figured out, but if I said I would and then I couldn't do it, I'd just get in more trouble.

Mr. Fairweather scribbled something on a notepad, tore off the sheet, folded it, and stapled it—*Whomp! Whomp!*—with the heel of his hand.

"Give this to Mrs. Belcher, please," he said.

I took my time walking back to the room, peeking into the note sideways, but I could only make out a few words like "tomorrow" and "not too" and "first." I stopped for a minute at the glass case in the hallway by the library where our class had a display of ancient Egyptian gods we shaped out of clay and painted.

Most kids' gods stood sideways and had animal heads and looked kind of stuck-up. But mine, Bes, was a fat, bow-legged, pop-eyed dwarf who stared right at you. I'd painted him yellow and orange, and he turned out great.

Bes. Snake-eater and protector of children. A good-luck god who scared away monsters. Hmmmm. It was worth a try. I held Drog up to the glass.

Nothing. So much for help from the gods.

I scuffed home alone through the sidewalk leaves, Drog in my pocket, trying to figure out what was happening to me. *Use your head, Parker. Either the impossible is true—the only puppet that ever talked on its own has just attached itself to your hand and won't let go—or else . . . what?*

A nightmare? It would have to be the longest bad dream a kid ever had. Was somebody playing a mean trick on me by remote control or something? If so, how? And why? As far as I knew, I didn't have any enemies.

What if I was out of my mind? Could it happen just like that? I was pretty sure I was normal up to the minute I put

Drog on, but maybe if you're really insane you don't even know it. They say you're crazy if you start hearing voices that aren't there. Drog's voice *was* there, though, because other people could hear it too. They just thought it was me talking. So was everybody else crazy?

Whoever Drog was, he did talk, and the only one who knew that was me, his prisoner. I needed to get free from him and *then* figure him out. Or not. Just get him off, that was the main thing.

chapter four

"Do you ever wash your pants, Boy? There are some nasty bits in your pocket I don't appreciate having my nose shoved into."

I frowned into the bathroom mirror.

"My name isn't Boy, it's Parker," I said.

"Whatever."

I rubbed my forehead to erase the frown marks, but I could still see them. Before Drog, the only thing different about me was my hair. It's plain brown, like a lot of people's, but it's real curly and, well, it's big. Drives my dad crazy, but Mom just says, "How come boys always get the curls?" Kids at school tease me and call me The Mop, but I think they kind of like it. Anyway, having big hair was nothing compared to going around with a puppet stuck on your hand.

Getting undressed was hard. I pretended my arm was broken. Even people with one arm in a cast have to get dressed and undressed, don't they? It took a long time.

Usually I take showers, and never in the daytime, but I climbed into our bathtub, one of those old ones with feet like animal claws. Maybe if I couldn't pull Drog off, I could take a bath and soak him off. I turned on the faucets.

But Drog said, "Drog doesn't bathe. You will keep me out of the water."

I held him out of the tub like he said to, but it made me mad. My last idea. If I couldn't soak him off, I was going to have to tell Mom—"Hey, Mom, I've got this talking puppet glued to my hand"—and get her all upset. Nobody had ever actually said so, but it was my job not to give her any worries.

I couldn't keep hiding Drog in my pocket. But if I did stick him under the water, he'd yell at me.

So what? Why should I take orders from him?

I hate this, I thought. I reached over and tried again to rip him off in one motion. As usual, he was too fast for me. He squeezed, hard.

"If you're so keen on taking something off, you might start with that ridiculous wig."

"It's not a wig. That's my hair."

"More's the pity."

I slumped down in the water, my Drog hand still up. "How do you do it, Drog?" I said. "How do you keep me from pulling you off?"

"Ha! Sheer willpower, Boy. Lots of it. You think I don't know what you would do with me if you could get me off your hand?"

"But *somebody* took you off. Or else how'd you end up in the—"

"Somebody is not you. We will not discuss it."

His green face hung over the edge of the bathtub, grinning that mocking grin. I pictured him not just floating off my hand in the water, but getting sucked down the drain headfirst. He was too big, but maybe that meant he'd get stuck. Even better!

I plunged him under, then flipped him so I couldn't see his face. I counted to three. To ten. Thirty. Was he letting go? Sixty.

A stony feeling crept up my chest as I realized what I was saying in my head. *Drown. Drown.* I didn't just want him to soak off. I wanted him to die.

Eighty. One hundred. I quit counting. If only I could lie in the warm bath forever and not think about what I had just done.

Finally, though, the water felt cold even when I scrunched down. I turned Drog back over.

"Well, now we know where we stand, don't we?" he snarled. "You had better get me dry, and quickly, or I will keep you up all night coughing."

I sighed and hauled myself out of the tub, pulled the plug chain, and toweled myself off as well as I could with a wet puppet on one hand. Then I set Mom's hair dryer on warm and aimed it at Drog. I wished I had a third hand so I could hold my nose, because Drog, wet, smelled like some old brown medicine you wouldn't want to take.

"Ah, that's more like it," he shouted over the dryer's whine. "This feels like the breeze off the desert in Kartoon the time the emir and I journeyed to the oasis there. Imagine a dozen chieftains with their retainers arriving on camels, and the desert abloom with colorful tents! We dined on figs and grape leaves, and of course there were the most beautiful dancing girls . . . ."

Did he say retainers? Would chieftains on camels wear braces on their teeth?

"Parker?" Mom called up the stairs. "Who's that you're talking to up there?"

"Uh, nobody, Mom, just talking—"

"Nobody? Drog is nobody? Where are your manners, Boy?" Drog said. "It's time you introduced me to the lady of the house!"

Did I have any choice?

It was hard to pull my clothes back on one-handed with my skin all spongy from the bath and me shaking inside and outside.

I crept downstairs with Drog, still slightly damp, in my pocket.

Mom had her back turned, stirring something on the stove, so I slid into my chair.

We live in a big old house that Dad still calls The Barn. Ever since he moved to Moline, Mom and I have been eating in the kitchen instead of the dining room. It's kind of cozy and kind of lonely. I still miss Dad, even though he would make me sit up straight and eat my french fries with a fork.

Funny, he always wanted to live in a house where everything was tidy and put away, a house with a few nice things sitting out on tables, like something out of a magazine. Now he does. Our house is more like something out of a book. Mom orders handmade stuff from around the world out of catalogs—baskets and bowls and carvings—and they're all over the place. My favorite is a carved wooden box from Peru that hangs on the wall in the kitchen. It has two doors that open out, and inside there's a workshop full of carved carvers carving more little workshops to hang on the wall, with carvers inside each of them, carving even tinier workshops. One time I tried looking at it through a magnifying glass, but I still couldn't see any end to the carving, and for some reason that made me happy.

Supper was spaghetti. Definitely a two-hander. I tried to scoot a bunch on my fork one-handed and look normal doing it.

Mom stopped eating to watch.

"So, Parker," she said, "you've been going around with one hand in your pocket since yesterday. Would that have anything to do with a message I got today from Mr. Fairweather? Some problem with a hand puppet?"

I worked Drog out of my pocket and held him up.

Mom flinched. "Kind of homely-looking isn't it?"

"Careful what you say, Mom."

"Is this the one you and Wren were arguing about?"

"Uh-huh. We found him in a trash can at the junk yard." The minute I said "trash can" I felt Drog squeeze.

"Hmmm," Mom said. "And you have a name for him?"

"He told me to call him Drog."

"He told you. Really."

"It's true, Mom! I put him on and he just started talking. I don't know how."

"Well, let's discuss that after supper. Put him away for now so you won't get spaghetti on him."

I forced myself to smile. "Maybe he likes spaghetti."

"Don't be silly. Take it off until after supper."

"I can't, Mom."

"You're not at school now, Parker. Take it off, please."

"I can't. I CAN'T!" I yelled.

Mom pushed back her chair and stared hard at me. "What's this *really* all about?"

"I told you. He won't *let* me take him off. And he talks whenever he feels like it. I can't stop that either. Mom, do I lie to you?"

She shook her head. "No. You don't always tell me everything, but no, you don't lie. That's what—"

"Then believe me."

She wiped her hands with her napkin. "I want to, Parker. I'm just . . . I'm trying to make sense of what you're saying. You don't make it talk?"

"No. I don't even know half of what he's talking about. And he's bossy. And rude."

Drog squeezed hard.

Mom started massaging the back of her neck. "Does it—he talk to anyone else? Wren?"

"No, because she called him a doll. And now she's barely talking to me. She thinks I'm making it up."

"And you can't take him off . . . because he won't let you? May I try?"

I held out my Drog hand, and she tugged on his bald green head.

"If at first you don't succeed, perhaps skydiving is not for you!" Drog said.

Mom frowned. She thought it was me saying that.

"Relax your hand, now."

"I am, Mom. See what I mean?"

Mom let go. "Oh, Parker. Why didn't you tell me about this right away?"

Good question. Why didn't I? "I guess . . . I wanted to take care of it."

"Well, that doesn't—that would be good. Do you have some ideas?"

"Not right now."

"I know," she said, pushing away from the table. "Let's just cut him off with scissors."

"Mom . . . we can't cut. . . . something that talks."

She rubbed the sides of her forehead in little circles. "Are you sure you want me to leave this up to you?"

I wasn't. I nodded.

"But what about school, Darling? Mr. Fairweather says you'll get detention if you still have it on tomorrow."

"I'll be okay, Mom," I said.

My spaghetti was getting cold and sticky. Mom cut it in pieces for me the way she used to when I was little.

"Looks like worms," Drog muttered.

How come I never noticed before?

chapter five

The phone rang. Dad. He talked to Mom first.

In the summer Dad drives down from Moline every other Saturday to pick me up for the weekend, but during the school year he mostly just calls and I don't see him much. Except when he makes a special trip to take me to the dentist. I guess he thinks Mom wouldn't remember to do that. Mom's a free spirit, he says, and he doesn't mean that as a compliment.

Mom looked up over the phone at me and shook her head. She didn't say anything to him about Drog. Then it was my turn.

"Hello, Son. What's new?"

"Nothing much." *I've just got a sarcastic green puppet superglued to my hand, that's all.*

"What have you been doing lately?"

How lately? "Oh, hanging out with Wren."

"Don't you ever play with the boys? Soccer or something?"

Here we go. "Sometimes. At school."

By "playing" Dad means going around with a bunch of boys and doing whatever they do. Or joining a team. But doesn't playing mean doing whatever you want? I like to decide what to do when the time comes, just fool around and make things up. Wren's like that too. And she's fun and easy to be with. At least before Drog she was.

Dad thinks I should have dozens of friends. He's got about a hundred programmed into his phone. He doesn't even count Wren, because she's a girl.

". . . done your homework yet, Parker?" Dad was saying.

"Um, no, but I've just got some English and math. No tests."

"I loved math when I was a kid."

"Yeah, I know," I said. *And I bet I know exactly what you're going to say next: the great thing about math—*

"The great thing about math is, every problem has a solution," he said.

I put the phone on speaker and doodled on the message pad. A boy with curly hair and a banana in each ear.

"Here's a story problem for you," Drog said. "If Parker gets a dollar for each time his dad tells him he loved math—"

Dad cleared his throat. "Did you say something, Parker?"

I stuffed Drog into my pocket.

"I said . . . I got an A in art. We made Egyptian gods out of clay. I made the god Bes. Mine's the bes', get it?"

There was silence for a moment. "Well, good. Put your mother back on, please. I'll talk to you again next week."

"Okay."

I didn't stick around to hear Mom's end of the conversation. Her voice always sounded tired talking to Dad. I hauled my book bag upstairs.

"Now, let's see, where were we?" Drog said.

"We?"

"Aha, you speak French?"

"No, I—"

"Do you speak any languages at all, Boy? Other than this clumsy English, I mean?"

"No." *And I barely get Bs in English.*

"Well, I suppose that would be too much to expect in these dreary times. Oh, the stories the emir and I used to tell together! And his son! Now there was a boy I could respect. Each day we acted out the most elegant tales in different languages: Farsi, Arabic, Svengali, Gelato—"

"Drog, I . . . I've got stuff to do for tomorrow."

With my free arm, I swung my book bag onto my desk, reached in for my English 6 book, and stared at my way-overdue assignment.

"Let me see," Drog said.

I brought my Drog hand up next to the book.

"English. Excuse me, you do speak English, don't you?" Drog said.

"Yes, but—"

"Then surely to study English is a ridiculous waste of your time."

"Oh, right! Tell that to Mrs. Belcher!"

Drog snickered. "Why would I tell anything to anyone named—ha-ha!—Belcher? What a disgusting name."

I made up a few quick sentences, then turned to my math problems. Drog peered at the page.

"What rubbish!" he said after a minute. "This book is based on erroneous principles. It can only confuse you."

"You're the one who's confusing me! Why do you talk like that, anyway? 'This book is based on erroneous principles.' Why don't you just say what you mean?" I scribbled any old answers and slammed the book shut.

"You don't learn real mathematics from books anyway," Drog said. "Why, you should have been with the emir and me the time we journeyed up the Silk Road to meet his good friend Cue-ball Khan of Mongolia. That was no ordinary khan, believe me, because he was seven feet tall. What a grand impression he made, coming through the mountain pass, seated in a carved jade saddle, the weight of which only one horse in Mongolia could bear!"

I'd have covered my ears, but I only had one hand. I wanted to choke his skinny neck with that one.

"Cue-Ball's right-hand man was a mathematician named Zed, who measured the distance between stars and used the numbers to predict when it would be a good time for the khan to sell horses or take another wife or go to war. You see, Boy? You should quit school and travel the world with me. Now *that* would be an education."

I jammed him into my pocket and headed downstairs to drop my backpack by the door.

Mom was still on the phone, but not with Dad.

"No, Nicole, I don't think it's the imaginary friend thing . . ."

I crouched down on the step to listen.

"After all, he's eleven now, almost eleven and a half. Besides, it doesn't seem to be a friend at all. That's what's got me worried. . . . I know, but he's always been such a level-headed kid, even through the divorce. . . . Yes, apparently he even slept with it on. Do you think . . . I hate to hear him talking to himself. . . . Well, he *is* answering back. . . . Oh I'm sure you're right. That's what Mr. Fairweather said. No sense overreacting."

What if Mom knew I tried to drown Drog? Would she think she was overreacting then?

I uncrouched and tiptoed back up the stairs, avoiding squeaky number four.

That night I managed to sleep all night, but Drog still haunted me. I dreamed I looked up into the puppet sleeve to see what was in there besides my hand. But as soon as I lifted the edge, a hollow voice that came from all around me said, "Are you sure?" Then there was this sucking, whooshing feeling and I was completely inside, floating alone in a huge darkness, with Drog and the glove way out there somewhere. I tried to touch down or reach out, but there was no floor or side, no up or down.

I held my breath, because the darkness around me wasn't empty, exactly. It was full of mist. A white mist of . . . loneliness. I couldn't tell if that was Drog's, or mine, or everybody's in the whole world, but I was desperate not to breathe any in. I remember thinking, *This is forever.*

Noooooooooooooooo, I screamed, but no sound came out.

I woke in my bed, cold with sweat from that horrible dream, and pulled the comforter up under my chin. The iron radiator clanked, and a faint pink morning light began to color my room with relief. I even laughed to see Drog back to normal size on my hand and to hear him snoring.

He woke up then and acted like he'd been awake first.

"What's so funny?" he said. "Get up and get going, Boy. Amuse me."

chapter six

"Hey, Parker," Charlie Sloat, a fifth-grader, called out. "What you got in your pocket? You playing with something in there?"

Everybody who could hear, which was just about everybody on the playground, cracked up laughing and came over. My face flamed. I pulled Drog out.

"Take it off," Charlie yelled. "Take it all off!"

One of the girls said in a mocking voice, "He *can't*."

"Yuck!" Charlie said. "Gonna get finger jam!"

His friend Logan stepped up to look Drog over. "Is it true that puppet talks? For real?"

"Yeah."

"That is so cool! I'll give you ten dollars for it!"

"It is not cool! You don't want him, believe me. And you haven't got ten dollars."

"Have too."

"Logan, forget it. He only talks for me, anyway." I turned away.

"See, you're making it up. Liar!"

Bad enough to be teased by my sixth-grade class. But fifth-graders! Okay, so now if I left Drog out I was weird. And if I hid him in my pocket, everybody would think I was doing something embarrassing.

A stray soccer ball rolled by my feet, but I let it go on into the street. Why should I bother to kick it back?

Everyone *knows* there's no such thing as a talking puppet, right? So when I tell people I have one, do they say, "Oh, well, we must be wrong, tell us all about it, Parker?" Nooooo. They'd rather believe I'm lying or that there's something wrong with me. Instead of changing their minds about talking puppets, they change their minds about me. Even my mother. Even my best friend.

I guess telling the truth only works when you have something usual to say. But what else was I supposed to do? Pretend to be a liar or a weirdo like everybody thought?

Mrs. Belcher gave me in-room detention for coming to school with Drog on. Kind of an all-day time out. That way I could listen in and do my work behind the bookcases without distracting the class.

43

Wren floated a note down over the top of my bookcase cage:

Let's not stay mad, OK? Want to go see the new puppies at the Taylors' house after school?

Did I!

Neither of us have ever had a dog, because our moms are both allergic. Mom's allergies haven't bothered her much since Dad left, but when it comes to dogs, she says we've got enough to handle as it is, whatever that means. But Wren and I have gotten to know all the dogs in the neighborhood and we take them for walks sometimes. When one of them has a litter of pups, we like to go pick one out and pretend it's ours.

"Draw *me*," Drog said in art period. But Mrs. Belcher told us to draw something from memory, putting in as much detail as we could. I drew my left hand, because I wasn't sure I was ever going to see it again.

It was hard. I remembered the scar on my index finger I got from a firecracker. And the place on my thumb where I had a wart burned off. But how did the other fingers go? I could draw a hand, but not *my* hand. Already I forgot what it looked like. I gave up and drew Drog. I could do him without looking. That awful stare.

As soon as the last bell rang, I grabbed my book bag and waited at the door so I could catch Wren coming out before she changed her mind. The other kids steered around me like I was the wrong end of a magnet.

"*Vamos!*" Wren said, but she was smiling. It took me a minute to figure out she didn't mean "Go away," she meant "Let's go."

The Taylors' dog, Kona, was all brown, but the five white pups looked like someone had splashed a bucket of rust-colored paint over them. We picked one that nosed into things more than the others. Wren held him to her cheek for a minute, then handed him to me. I took him with my free hand.

With Wren being friendly again, and with a freckly, wriggly puppy on my lap gumming my finger, my chest eased up for the first time since Sunday at the junkyard. It felt like a month since Sunday.

But then Wren asked me, sort of in a whisper, "The puppet, what did you call it?"

My stomach twisted. "Drog."

"Drog. It didn't talk to you, did it? Not really?" She stroked the puppy's ear.

I wanted say, "No. I'm sorry I ever said that." But I had to say, "Yeah, Wren, he did. He still does."

She pulled her hand back. "Are you going to keep on doing this, then?"

"Doing what?"

"You know, leaving me out. Pretending you can't help it."

"Pretending? Why would I pretend?"

"I don't *know*," she wailed.

That made me mad. I was the one with the big problem, so why was she upset? All she had to do was believe me and help me think.

"It's not so great for me, you know," I snapped at her. "I feel like I'm *his* puppet!"

"Well, don't be then. Be you. Take that stupid thing back to the junkyard."

I didn't answer. Whatever you could say about Drog, he wasn't stupid.

She took the puppy from me and said she wanted to go. I felt like I had a chunk of apple stuck halfway down my throat.

The minute I got home and shut the door to my room, I pulled Drog back out of my pocket. Maybe I just wanted to see how bad I could make myself feel.

"That's right," he said. "Spend the whole afternoon having your selfish fun. And what about me? I'm supposed to just stand on my head in your pocket while you play? With puppies? How excruciatingly cute!"

Selfish? Look who's talking.

"I thought Wren would like it better if I kept you out of sight, that's all," I said. "Why won't you talk for her, anyway?"

"Humph! One has to have some standards. Good riddance, I say!"

46

"But Wren's my friend."

He sighed like he was trying to be patient. "Don't you see, Boy? Now that you have Drog, you don't need friends."

Those words sucked the air right out of my mouth and started something roiling in my stomach, forcing its way to my throat. I ran to the toilet and threw up everything I ever ate.

I dragged back to my room then and fell onto my bed. Squiggly things danced around under my eyelids, and I could hear my blood rushing around inside, knocking against my skin. My bedside clock went *Chick tick chick tick chick tick*. A little torture machine.

Then my eyes shot open.

Suddenly I knew what to do about Drog! How to make him stop talking, anyway. And Wren actually gave me the idea.

I took him out again.

"That's more like it, Boy," he said. "Let's do something interesting."

"Ha! You can't do anything, Drog. You're just a . . . *doll*."

He stalled for about one minute, and then he laughed. "Ha-ha! Good one. You're a bit sharper than I thought. Won't work, though. You know why?"

The aftertaste of throw-up burned my throat. "Why?"

"Because you're not that girl. I know you know I'm not a doll."

"I hate you, Drog!" I said.

"Now you're talking! Hate me all you like, Boy. It makes no difference. You and I were meant for each other."

I glared at him. He glared back until I blinked. Then, although I would have given anything not to, I started crying.

I'd never felt so hopeless, except maybe the morning Dad and Mom told me they were getting divorced, but they would both always love me, blah blah. That same tight twisting in my chest that crying couldn't help, but I had to cry anyway.

"Get lost, Drog!" I said, catching my breath, "Go . . . go back to whatever dark hole you crawled out of. I wish I'd never seen your pukey green face, I wish—"

"Mercy, get a grip! Bad enough that I'm stuck with someone so awfully young and boring and ungrateful, but a crybaby? This is too much."

Fresh anger stopped my tears. "What do you mean *you're* stuck with *me*? If you don't like it, at least *you* can do something about it!"

"Think so? Haul your head out of the wishing well now, Boy, and blow your nose. I don't care to lie around listening to you snivel and regurgitate."

I wanted to blow my nose all right. On him.

"Hmmm," he went on. "What could we do that would be exciting? Maybe we should get involved with something . . . illicit. A smuggling operation perhaps. Not guns, of course— too messy. Diamonds, rhinoceros horns, art objects, that sort of thing. You meet the most interesting people."

"Smuggling? In Ferrisburg?"

Drog sighed. "You have a point. How can you bear to live here, thousands of miles from the bounding main? From anywhere, actually. Oh, If only you knew the adventures I've had! I assume you've heard of the mysterious Ruby Yacht of Omar Khayyam?"

It did sound kind of familiar, but I didn't know where from.

"The Ruby Yacht would have been the eighth wonder of the world if it hadn't disappeared. That boat had a will of its own, never liked to stay long in one place. I am proud to say it was once my privilege to . . . liberate it."

Oh great. Another story, with Drog the hero.

"I was then in the employ of a sultan who coveted that fabled yacht more than life itself. But at the time it belonged to Omar Khayyam of Persia. My job was to distract Omar with stories while the sultan's agents bribed the crew with gold and sailed Omar's gleaming white pleasure boat, its deck and masts studded with Burmese rubies, away in the dark of night.

"When we presented the ruby yacht to the sultan, he ordered a great feast and entertained us with dancing girls, hundreds of them. What a night! But the sultan himself only wanted to spend time on the yacht, sailing it back and forth on his private lake. Then one day he died. And the next day the yacht vanished."

"What happened to it?"

"Who knows? Perhaps it is roaming the world still. Shall we go in search of it?"

I looked him in the eye. "Did you take it, Drog?"

"Would I be here talking to you if had? No, the sultan lost interest in puppets long before he died—"

"So he gave you to the emir, right?"

"You have too good a memory, Boy. But perhaps . . . Ferrisburg also has some dancing girls?"

"I don't think so."

"You don't think so. Must Drog play with puppies, then? What sorry fortune. I might be content if I could have dancing girls."

And maybe you'd shut up for a while.

I leaned over to the computer. "Wait," I said. "Let me type in 'dancing girls' and see what happens."

"I don't want to write to them, Boy. I want to watch them."

"Shhh."

I couldn't believe what popped up on the screen. Eight squares like windows, and in each one a naked lady shaking her behind all over the place. You couldn't see their heads.

"Aha!" Drog said.

But they were animations, not real people. After a while everything repeated and you could tell which way they were going to move next. It got boring. Even Drog thought so.

"Let's see some real dancing girls," he said.

I checked on the links. Go-go. Hootchy-kootchy. I clicked on Belly Dance.

"Now we're getting somewhere," Drog said as pictures of long-haired women with bare middles and sparkling tops and skirts came on the screen. "Let's see them dance."

But we couldn't. They wanted you to order a belly-dancing video for $14.99, so the site just had photos. I switched back to the naked bottoms. I didn't hear Mom come to the doorway.

"Parker, what on earth are you looking at?"

I closed out as fast as I could and jammed Drog into my pocket. "Um, nothing, Mom."

She sat down on the edge of my bed. "Parker, I need to talk to you."

"Sorry, Mom. That was kind of an accident. I won't watch that stuff again."

"It's not that," she said.

What, then? Mom acted funny. Like she was trying hard not to act funny. She examined her fingernails for a minute.

"I've been talking with Mr. Fairweather and Mrs. Belcher. I think I've convinced them that you're not trying to be disruptive. So we made a deal. They're going to let you sit back in with the class tomorrow, even with the puppet on."

"Good." I waited for the "but." If there was a deal, there had to be a "but."

"But there's one condition. You're going to go see a doctor—Dr. Mann. He's a child psychologist, a good one."

My stomach turned, even with nothing left in it. Great. Now everyone thought I was sick. In the head.

"A psychologist? Does he know anything about puppets?"

"I don't know, but he knows a lot about children."

Uh-oh. "Do I have to go?"

"No, but I'd like you to."

Same thing.

The minute she left the room, Drog said, "Order those dancing girls for me. If I'm to be confined to a life of boredom, it's the least you can do."

"Forget it, Drog," I muttered. "I only get five dollars allowance."

Actually I had lots more money saved in my drawer. But why should I spend it on a puppet-monster who loved to hate me?

Child psychologist. I prayed for appendicitis.

chapter seven

Mom picked me up Friday after school. She still drives the old Taurus that used to be Dad's car, our family car.

Some of the best fun I had with Dad when I was little was when he drove me places. Just us. I didn't care where. I thought being an engineer meant he could drive a train, so as soon as we got in the car he'd twist his hat backwards and pretend to toot the whistle. He told me stories while he drove, and I told him some back. We sang camp songs he learned when he was a kid—*Black socks, they never get dirty. The longer you wear 'em, the blacker they get!*—and made up silly new verses. Dad would slap the steering wheel, laughing, and forget all about trying to teach me the right way to do things.

All that was back when I still called him Daddy. For a long time after he left, I didn't call him anything.

Dad drives a silver Lexus now. Quiet. No crumbs.

My appointment wasn't until four, but Mom drove straight there. Because you never know, she said, we might get held up at the crossing by one of those endless freight trains and be late. She didn't usually worry so much about being on time.

We were way early. A man sat on one of the two couches in Dr. Mann's waiting room, reading *Outdoor Life* and crossing and uncrossing his legs. We sat down on the other couch near a wall of rippley glass bricks. If you looked just right at it, you could see yourself about a thousand times. I flipped through a beat-up copy of *Highlights* with all the puzzle answers filled in.

The door opened, and the doctor came out with a girl about my age who'd been crying. A lot. What went on in there? Dr. Mann smiled and shook hands with the man. Then he turned to me.

"Please come in."

Mom waved me her you-can-do-it wave, and I went.

The inside of Dr. Mann's office looked pretty much like the waiting room. It even had one glass-brick wall. Two round wooden tables—one low, with little-kid-sized chairs, and one regular with regular chairs—were the only furniture besides his desk.

Dr. Mann invited me to sit across the regular-sized table from him and told me I could call him Dr. M.

"This is a special place, Parker," he said. "Usually, whenever we are not alone, we have to be careful what we say. It's part of getting along together. But in this room, with me, you can say whatever you feel like saying. You won't shock or hurt anyone. And no one else will know."

We sat there for a while. I counted my reflections in the glass bricks.

"I understand you have a friend," Dr. Mann said, finally.

A *friend?*

"Did you bring him with you?"

Oh, he meant Drog. I showed him my Drog hand.

"He's not my friend."

"I see."

"He's bossy. And rude. And he's conceited." Drog crunched my hand.

Dr. M. nodded. "And a friend would be someone who—"

I thought about Wren. Before.

"—someone you like who likes to do the things you do, someone you trust, someone who believes what you—"

No! I wasn't going to start bawling right there. I stuck Drog back in my pocket and swallowed hard.

If Dr. Mann noticed, he pretended he didn't. "Parker, do you think it's important that Drog is a man?"

I shrugged. I didn't even want to think about a girl Drog. Yuck.

"Have you ever been in a play?" he said. "At school, maybe?"

"No. I've seen some plays, though."

"Good. When someone acts in a play they pretend they're somebody else, right?"

I nodded.

He leaned forward and rested his hands on the table. His fingernails were perfect moons.

"Let's pretend for a minute that you and I are in a play that has two characters: a boy and his father. Why don't you be the father and I'll be the boy? What would the father say to the boy?"

"I don't know. It depends."

It was starting to feel too warm in the room.

"Well, suppose he hasn't seen the boy for a while, and he calls him on the telephone."

That was easy. "Hello, Son."

"Hello, Dad," the doctor said. "When are you coming to see me?"

"I don't think the boy would say that," I said.

"Why not?"

"Because he knows the dad's not coming."

"I see. And that's because—"

Suddenly I started chattering about how my dad moved to Moline when I was seven and how I hated going back and forth between my parents and got sick every time and how after a couple of years they said I could stay home except every other weekend in the summer when I would go to Dad's. How I used to have this daydream that our house on Prairie Street actually belonged to me and if Mom and Dad couldn't get along, *they* could take turns coming and going. Or else we could all live in the house, but Dad would have a separate room with an outside door and we could visit back and forth and maybe all have supper together sometimes.

I even told how Dad got married again, and how he and his other wife, who was nice enough but nothing like Mom, had a little baby called Shanna I'd only seen a few times, and how even I had to admit it was all over between Mom and Dad.

I sank back in my chair. "So the boy knows the dad's not coming."

That was a sad thing to say out loud, but I felt like a rubber band let go when I said it. And all the time Dr. M. gave me his complete attention.

"It's natural to blame your father for the divorce," he said.

"What?" I said. "I mean, what's divorce got to do with this puppet?"

"Maybe nothing. Maybe a lot. What do you think?"

"I don't see how."

"Maybe you could take Drog off now?"

"I don't know."

"Let's try."

"He'll yell at me."

"But once we get him off, maybe he won't be able to say anything. Try it?"

I slid my pointer finger inside and pulled, but nothing happened.

"Boy," Drog said, "let's get out of here."

The doctor cleared his throat. "We won't be much longer, Parker. Here, let me help you."

He circled my wrist with his thumb and finger and tugged on Drog's head and hands with his other hand. His grip was gentle.

"Just relax, Parker. Relax your hand."

"I am. It's Drog who won't let go."

Dr. M. sat back.

"I see. Apparently this is one determined puppet. Well, don't worry about it. In fact, try not to worry about anything at all. For now, just ignore Drog and do the things you want with or without him, all right? Ah, our time's up. I'll see you next week."

"How'd it go?" Mom asked on the way out.

"He seemed nice," was all I said. I'd blabbed enough for one day.

"You know what makes your life such a zero, Boy?" Drog said when we got home. "You spend your days with fools."

"Dr. M.? He was okay. At least he believed me."

"You think so? 'Ignore Drog,' ha! What ignorance! When it's time to see that Dr. Mann again, you and I will have a previous engagement."

Friday. What was I going to do for a whole weekend without Wren?

That night wasn't actually so bad. Mom brought out a video she checked out from the library where she works. She likes movies about other places and times, and I like adventure, so she chose *October Sky*. It's about this small-town kid named Homer back in the nineteen-fifties who gets all excited after the Russians put up Sputnik, the first satellite, and starts building his own rockets. Some of his friends get into it, too, but he is the leader, and after a couple of impressive blow-ups, he makes terrific rocket. He dreams of becoming a rocket scientist, and his mom is all for it. His dad, though, is counting on him to stay in Coalwood and work in the mine like him and his grandfather.

For a while, I almost forgot about Drog.

chapter eight

Saturday it poured. Way after Mom left for the library, I rolled out of bed and fixed myself some toast, dropping a couple of blobs of jelly on my foot.

"Ah. That would be toe jam, I presume," Drog said.

Then I just couldn't get started on anything, because everything needed Wren. It was like when there's a power failure and you keep forgetting and trying to switch on lights.

I could see nothing but rain out of every window. There were plenty of unfinished projects in the spare room, like the flying saucer I was trying to make out of a model-plane motor and two hubcaps I found. Things I'd built out of Legos, starting with the crocodile I made when I was seven, crammed the shelves where Dad used to keep his engineering notebooks in neat rows.

Maybe I could work on Wren's and my bird feeder, which was supposed to look like this Japanese castle. We had to buy bags of extra Legos from the thrift shop so we'd have enough whites.

I tried snapping a couple of bricks together, but they slipped and pinched my finger. I probably could do it, but it was hard. Too slow. No fun anymore. I needed two hands. Or a friend.

I wandered back into the living room and rewound the movie from the night before. This time, watching the kids make rockets and set them off just reminded me of all the things I couldn't do anymore. And Homer's arguments with his dad made me shut the thing off.

"You've got a rocket in your pocket," Drog said.

Dad. I was going to have to get free from Drog before Dad found out about him, but how? When Dad had a problem he couldn't solve, he wrote it out, and he always came up with an answer.

I took a pencil and notepad from Mom's desk and wrote: *I need to get this talking puppet off my hand.* Then I drew little arrows out from the problem the way Dad does, pointing to possible solutions. Arrow: *pull him off.* Arrow coming out of that arrow: *squeezes harder and stays on.* More arrows for cutting and soaking and even *pretend he's not there,* with arrows coming out of them all leading to "stays on." Dad's arrows led to answers, mine just took me back to the problem. I must be stupid. I scribbled a picture of me, cross-eyed.

After studying the phone for a while, I picked it up and called Wren.

Her mom answered.

"I'm sorry, Parker. Wren's not here right now. She's at a friend's house."

"Oh, that's right," I said, making myself feel even dumber. "Thanks."

A friend's house.

"You see?" Drog said.

I scuffed into the kitchen. Wren and I always had plans. For the day and for the future. As soon as we were old enough to drive, we were going to put together a whole car from junkyard parts and go on a long trip out west together, exploring towns in the atlas that nobody ever heard of unless they lived close by, towns with names like Hurricane, Utah; Searchlight, Idaho; and, Wren's favorite, Horse Heaven, Oregon. And of course we'd collect lots of rocks along the way. We were really going to do it. We'd even saved some money.

I made a baloney sandwich and got mustard on my shirt. I don't especially like baloney, but the only way I was ever going to be able to eat peanut butter again was if somebody spread it for me. Pathetic.

Now what? If Wren wasn't home, maybe I could at least go over and hang around her dad's shop, even if I all I could do was watch. I missed the smell of fresh sawdust and turpentine and hot chocolate in the shop, the easy quiet while we worked or figured something out, and the feel of fresh-cut wood.

I wasn't sure I could face Mr. Rivera, though. He always called Wren "*Mi Corazon*," his heart. What if he thought I was doing something on purpose to upset her? He'd be mad at me too, and I couldn't take that.

"So what am I going to do all afternoon?" I said out loud.

"Well, something, I hope," Drog said, "or I shall scream with boredom."

"You? Am I supposed to feel sorry for you? Whose fault do you think it is that I can't do anything, anyway?"

"You want me to answer that?"

It was still dripping out, but I couldn't stand to stay home another minute. I hauled myself upstairs to my room and fished out three dollars from the money jar in my dresser. Then I took out another two.

I wormed into my jacket, tugged the left sleeve down over Drog, and headed for Cheapers downtown. They advertised paperbacks, comics, games, and "1,000 used videos—Great Selection!" Maybe I could at least get something to keep Drog busy so I could feel sorry for myself in peace.

The musty smell of old comics hit my nose the minute I walked into the store.

I glanced around. I was the only one in there except for an old man I didn't know who was browsing through the comics. Near that section was a roped-off corner lit up with a string of white Christmas-tree lights and a sign saying "Adult Videos." I glanced at the old man and at the guy behind the counter with the silver rings in his ears. Neither one was paying attention to me, so I made my way over there.

"Oh, looky, looky!" Drog said, checking out the cover pictures.

Plenty of dancers in that section, all right.

"Get me *The Exciting Art of Exotic Dance*," he said, "Or maybe *Strip Tease to Please*."

Probably just the thing to make him happy for a while. Darn!

"Drog, they'd never let me buy these. I don't think I'm even supposed to be looking at them."

"Ridiculous. Just slip one or two into your pocket No one will know. Good experience for you."

I watched my hand reach out and actually had to remind myself, *That would be stealing.*

"Hey, dude," the counter guy said. "Looking for something in particular?"

I pulled my hand back and put Drog away. "Um. A video. On belly dancing."

The guy laughed. "Belly dancing? Hmmm. I think we've got a how-to over here in Exercise."

I looked it over a minute and shook my head.

"Oh. You don't want to do it, you want to watch it?"

"I just need a video with dancing girls in it."

He laughed again. "I bet you do. You crack me up, kid. Now, let me think. Should be plenty of red-hot dancing girls in *Road to Morocco*. Best I can do." He handed me the tape.

"How much you got?"

"Five dollars."

"Tell you what," the guy said. "You can have both videos for five dollars even."

"Okay, thanks."

"And come back when you get a little older. I'm sure I can find something interesting for you."

"It's not for me, it's for . . . somebody else."

"Rrrrright." He wrote out the sales slip and handed me the package. "There you go. Enjoy!"

The Cheapers bag was see-through, so as soon as I got outside, I stuffed it inside my jacket. The last thing I needed was to have to explain to anybody what I was doing downtown with a puppet on my hand, buying belly-dance videos.

I zipped the zipper up to my chin and looked up just in time to see a tall Japanese man coming out of the library. Must be the same guy Wren and I saw moving things into the old furniture store, I thought. I kept on looking at him because of the way he walked down the steps. So easy, like he was riding on an escalator. He didn't seem to have things nagging his mind like everybody else on the street. Like me.

I wanted more than anything to follow him and see where he went, but my feet stayed velcroed to the spot, and then he was gone. All the way home, I kicked the dried leaves ahead of me on the sidewalk.

"What did you do today, Parker?" Mom asked at supper.

"Not much. Went downtown. Came home."

"I expected to find you working on something or other in the spare room."

I frowned and waved Drog at her.

"Oh, Parker, you love to make things. I'd hate to see you give that up."

I shoved away from the table to go upstairs. Mom started to follow me.

"Parker?"

"It's okay," I said. "I've got . . . a project. Um, Mom, did you happen to see a Japanese man at the library today?"

"What? Oh, not today. I was cataloging in the back. I know the man you mean, though. He comes in often. I always notice him because he's quiet, the way people used to be in libraries. It's refreshing."

I spent a couple of hours copying just the dancing parts from the video onto my computer so I could play them over and over for Drog.

I was dumb if I thought that was going to keep him happy. He watched it once, made a yawning noise, and said, "Mmmm. Like watching soup cool."

I turned on the TV.

Mom looked in on me to say good night. "You know, your dad used to make things, too. Before he got so busy. You probably don't remember that little plane. . . ."

I did, though. It was made of real light wood. You turned the propeller and twisted a rubber band, then let go and it flew all over the yard.

"Yeah, I remember."

"Wonder whatever happened to it?"

"I probably broke it," I said. But then I remembered. One day a couple of years ago I blew it up with a firecracker. For no particular reason. I just wanted to see something explode.

I had finally figured out how to imagine doing my bedtime wooden shapes routine one-handed, but that night whenever I got something to go together, it blew apart and woke me up.

On Sunday I decided to go to the junkyard without calling Wren and see if maybe she'd just be there. She wasn't. It was plain cold out, one of those November days that turns everything the color of steel.

Our birdcage was gone, and the junk was all just junk except for one incredible new thing: a whole freight car off its wheels. I wished Wren could see it. The door was open, so I scrambled up inside. It smelled sour in there, like spilled vinegar. A flattened packing box lay on the floor. Someone had slept on it and left. Probably too cold for them. Or too lonely. I tightened the string on my jacket hood and headed back home.

―――――

When Dad called that night I knew what to expect. Mom said she had to tell him what was happening. I guessed I could see why.

"Hello, Dad."

"I understand you've been in some trouble at school," he said in his trying-to-be-patient voice. "Making up stories. Getting sent to the office."

"I didn't make anything up."

"Well then, explain this talking puppet business to me."

How? "Okay. I found a puppet and put him on my hand, and he talks, and he won't let me take him off."

"Do you expect me to believe that?"

"No." I pressed the speaker button and doodled a picture of myself on the notepad.

"Look, Son, use your head. Whatever you're doing this for, it isn't worth it. In fact, it's a bad idea to let people think you're—"

"Crazy?"

"I was going to say strange."

"I can't help it." I drew branches growing out of my hair.

"You can't if you think you can't. Parker, there's something I want you to do. Two things, actually. First, give yourself a deadline by which this . . . thing has to be gone, and make up your mind that it will be—"

"Kind of like a wart?" I added a huge wart to my chin in the drawing.

"And second, I'd like you to sign up for boxing lessons and practice a little every day."

"Boxing takes two hands, Dad."

"Exactly."

"Okay, I'll think about it."

What else could I say? I handed the phone back to Mom.

Boxing again. The first Christmas after Dad left, he gave me a pair of boxing gloves and a punching bag. His idea of a present, not mine. Mom said he probably thought that without a dad around I might need to learn to defend myself. Trouble was, he never got around to getting the bag hung up in the garage. I put on the gloves a few times, but I never really used them, and after a while they got too small. Didn't he realize that? It was almost four years ago.

Besides, I got along fine. Boys at school sometimes got mad at each other, even wrestled or shoved each other around, but then it was over. We've never had any full-time bullies. Sometimes guys from the military school on the edge of town came around acting tough, but that was it.

I paced the living room, waiting for Mom to finish talking.

"Dad's always got all the answers," I said to her as soon as she hung up.

"Well, your dad's a reality guy," she said. "You're asking him to believe that a puppet talks."

"No. I'm asking him to believe *me*." *And you don't believe me, either. You're just trying to be nice about it.*

"He's probably trying to think what's best for you."

I punched the back of the arm chair with my free hand. "That's what I mean! Everybody thinks they know what's best for me. Why don't you all just leave me alone? That's what's best for me!"

Mom frowned and took hold of me by the shoulders. "Parker, I am giving you a huge benefit of the doubt here. You say you're doing as well as you can with this puppet business—"

"Right!"

"So I'm trying not to talk about it for a while, like Dr. Mann says, and let you work it out, but that's not easy. Give me some help, will you?"

I never did like having her mad at me, but this time she wasn't just mad, she looked really worried. About me. And whoever's fault this all was, it wasn't hers.

"Sorry I yelled," I said. "I didn't mean you."

"You sure about that?" Drog said to me on the way upstairs.

chapter nine

When an adult you don't know suddenly shows up on the playground at Monday recess, everybody thinks, "substitute." But, if this guy was a substitute, why wouldn't kids from his class either be hanging around him, trying to be his friend, or yelling and pushing each other to see what he'd do?

This man just stood off to the side, writing things in a notebook. He didn't look much like a teacher, either. More like a guy who used to play basketball back when he had more hair. A bunch of us asked Mrs. Belcher about him.

"Oh, that's Mr. Masterson," she said. "He taught here a few years ago, and now he works for the *Western Illinois Times*. He's gathering material for a series the magazine is doing on small-town schools."

"You mean he's going to write about us?" Wren asked.

"Not exactly. It's more about the school. He says he wants to observe a typical school day. So just do whatever you would usually do and ignore him."

But wherever I went on the playground, whether I was playing kickball with Gordy and the boys or just taking a drink from the fountain, the man went too, jotting things down. At afternoon recess, the same thing happened, so it was kind of hard to ignore him. If he wanted typical, he should definitely be ignoring me.

I guessed I could see why he would watch me, though. Writing about a school day had to be pretty boring, and most schools probably didn't have a kid with a bald green puppet on his hand.

I just wished he wasn't so interested. I could still play soccer and kickball even with Drog on my hand, and once a game got started, the kids kind of forgot about him and treated me as normal. I didn't need them to be reminded.

"Don't be a fool," Drog said. "I know a spy when I see one!"

───

"Now I get it, Parker!" Wren said as our class walked back to the room from library period. "Now I know what you're doing!"

"What?"

"This!" She showed me a book called *Voice Magic* and grinned like she'd just gotten an A in her worst subject. "You're trying to be a ventriloquist." Wren looks things up.

"Hey, man, what's a ven . . . quilotrist?" a low voice said from behind us. It was Big Boy, the oldest kid in class.

"Ventriloquist," Wren corrected him. "It's someone who pretends not to talk, but throws his voice to a dummy." Her eyes pointed at me "I'm going to learn how, too."

Great. Now she'd called Drog a dummy.

Big Boy looked confused.

"It's kind of an act," I said. "Somebody learns how to talk without moving their mouth. They make it seem like somebody or something else is talking. Like a puppet."

"Is that what you're doing?" Big Boy said. "It's an act?"

"No. It's not an act. I'm not making Drog talk."

Big Boy shook his head and walked ahead.

"I guess you wanted to keep your secret to yourself," Wren said. "But remember, we found that puppet together, so it's part mine too. You should at least let me have a turn."

"You didn't want him, Wren, remember? And now I couldn't give him to you if I tried."

You got it half right, Wren, I thought. *Somebody's a ventriloquist here, but it's Drog, not me.*

Drog cackled when I showed him the picture I drew in art of a boxer, all beat-up and punchy with a bloody cut over his eye, and a man in a business suit holding up the boxer's arm and saying, "That's my boy." Mrs. Belcher looked up. I didn't turn the picture in.

I'd better watch it, I thought, *or I'll end up in the Big B.M.* Bradley Military Institute. Adults say it's for boys who need more "structure." But kids all know it's where juvenile delinquents go, if their parents can afford it. It's a well-known secret that the older cadets there set up torture chambers to "initiate" the new kids after lights-out.

Dad once asked if I'd like to go to Bradley, as if it would be a good thing. Maybe he liked the short haircuts. Anyway, I didn't need him thinking of me as a kid who needs more "structure."

"Where are you taking me, may I ask?" Drog said when I got on my bike and headed downtown instead of home.

"To the Y."

"Y the Y?"

"They teach boxing there."

"Boxing? You want someone to knock some sense into you? I could do that, and you wouldn't even have to leave the house."

But I wasn't planning to sign up. I was just going down so I could tell Dad I tried.

The gym door made a kind of sucking sound as I dragged it open with my good hand. Inside, a class was finishing up. No kids, just some men with big wet patches on their shirts. It smelled like a bunch of old sneakers and wet dogs in there. I swallowed, went up to the instructor, and told him my dad wanted me to take boxing but I had a puppet on my hand that I couldn't take off. My voice came out kind of high. I showed him Drog.

"What the—" the man said. "Sorry, Son, I don't have time for this. Come back when you're through fooling with that thing."

Someone in the class called out, "I know, why don't you try kickboxing?" and everybody laughed, including Drog.

"Why do you let men you don't even know call you Son?" Drog asked.

I didn't feel like getting back on my bike right away. I didn't feel like doing much of anything, so I parked myself on a bench in the hall and tried to focus on my cheek mole. It's on the right side, and if I look as far to the right as I can make my eyes go, I can sometimes see it without looking in the mirror.

Just beyond the mole I could see someone looking at me. Looking, but not staring. A tall man. Japanese. The guy from the library steps. With his white shirt and wide black pants tied around the middle, he looked like a figure cut out of crisp paper. His eyes said *hello.*

And then he came over and sat down next to me. "Are you waiting for someone?"

"No. I don't know. I was trying to sign up for boxing."

"Do you want to box?"

"No. Besides, I can't."

"Oh?"

I showed him Drog. "I can't take him off."

"That's interesting."

Interesting?

"And I can't do much with him on."

"I see."

We were both quiet for a while. I could hear sneakers squeaking on the gym floor down the hall. Then the man said, "Some of my students are about to give a demonstration of aikido, a martial art. Would you like to see it?"

I nodded and followed him into a large room where a gray tumbling mat covered most of the floor. Some men and women dressed in loose white outfits knelt in a row on the mat with their hands on their knees, waiting. People in ordinary clothes sat in chairs on the other side of the room. The man in white and black led me over there. Then the kneelers all stood up and bowed to him and the demonstration began.

It was pretty amazing. One of them ran at somebody else as hard as they could, and the other person caught the attacker, tossing him through the air like a beanbag.

I tensed up, waiting for the thud, but the guy just landed and rolled and came up for more, like he enjoyed it. Several people attacked one person and the same thing happened. Then they switched and the attackers got thrown.

This must be some kind of stunt-actor training, I thought. It was like those old cartoons where the characters run off the edge of a cliff and crash to the ground, then get up and dust themselves off. Cool.

After a while the man—everyone in white called him Sensei—asked if anyone had questions. The woman sitting next to me asked what everybody else was wondering,

"Doesn't it hurt when you fall like that?"

Sensei smiled. "Not when you know how. Learning to fall is an important part of our training."

He went on to talk about aikido and how it had a special idea behind it: that you could learn to defend yourself without getting hurt or hurting anyone else.

"Ha! How can they call it a martial art if no one gets hurt?" Drog grumbled. "Looks like ballroom dancing to me."

When the demonstration was over, Sensei handed me a card. "If you think you'd like to try this," he said, "come to the dojo any evening between five and seven. Beginners usually come at five."

"The dojo?"

"It's our regular martial arts practice hall. You'll find our address on the card."

"What about—?" I asked, holding Drog up.

Sensei looked into me and said, "He's welcome, too."

"Don't you believe it," Drog muttered.

"I think I found something a lot more fun than boxing," I told Mom when I got home. "It's called aikido. It's a martial art."

"Oh. Like karate?"

"Sort of. Here's where they practice." I handed her the card.

"Hmmmm, that must be where the old Montgomery Furniture store used to be. That's not far from the library. When are the classes?"

"Every day at five. Can I go tomorrow?"

"Well yes, sure. Aikido, hmm?"

That night it was even harder than usual to concentrate on my homework, and not because Drog kept yakking at me. I couldn't stop thinking about those people in white rolling on the floor and throwing each other across the room.

If I had some clay, I thought, and if I had both hands, I could make some aikido figures. I drew a few instead, flying through the air. Smiling.

I got into bed and closed my eyes, focusing on my wood shapes. Spirals and rods turned into roots and branches in my mind, then came together to form a huge tree extending as far as I could see.

PART II

Learning to Fall Down

chapter ten

I got to the dojo early, wearing baggy pants and a sweat-shirt faded to the color of strawberry Jell-O powder. The old Montgomery Furniture sign still showed on the storefront window, but I couldn't see in. I stretched my sweatshirt sleeve down to cover Drog and opened the door.

The thick white paper covering the storefront windows glowed from the late afternoon light trying to shine through. There was no furniture at all inside, just a clean, bare wood floor, partly covered by one big tumbling mat and one small one off to the side.

An older girl, dressed in white with an orange cloth tied around her waist, knelt on the floor barefoot, facing a scroll of swirly black writing on the front wall. I took off my shoes and socks too. The floor felt cool and smooth.

Pretty soon other kids came in, and we waited off to the side without talking. The place was just naturally quiet and calm. I couldn't believe I was still in Ferrisburg. It was like being snowed in. And I was about to learn the secret of flying through the air without getting hurt, like those people I saw at the Y!

Sensei entered through a side door and bowed to us. Right away the girl in white bowed back, and we copied her.

"Let's begin with a concentration exercise," Sensei said.

"Let's get out of here," Drog mumbled in my sleeve. "I believe we have a previous—"

But I was concentrating already, more awake than I ever felt in school. I pulled my sleeve down more.

"I see most of you are new," Sensei said, so let's begin with our one-point, not because it is for beginners, but because it is the most important thing. In aikido we aim to create harmony. To do that we must always balance and focus, putting our attention on our one-point, our center. Yours is located directly below your navel, about two inches below. Know where that point is and put your mind there as often as you can."

I had to smile. Finding my center would be easy. Because two inches below my belly button was my only other mole.

"Now place your hand over your center and breathe slowly in and out."

I covered my mole with my right hand.

"As you breathe, say one-point one-point . . ."

We all breathed and mumbled the words.

"Good," Sensei said. "Do this many times a day until you can do it without using your hand or saying the words out loud.

"That's it. Remember, whenever you need to balance or calm yourself, on or off the mat, repeat, 'one-point one-point.' That is the beginning of your practice. Tomorrow you will learn the first roll."

Next he and the girl with the orange sash demonstrated that first roll, plus a lot of throws and rolls that he would be teaching in the coming months. Sensei kept saying how important it was to focus and relax. Finally he taught us five different stretches we could do at home and before class to stay flexible and avoid injury. He explained how to sign up if we decided to and measured each of us for the uniform, the *gi*. Then he bowed to dismiss us.

Drog pestered me on the way home. "One-point, gunpoint. I'm not taking a fall, no matter what Pansy says!"

"It's not Pansy, Drog, it's Sensei, and besides, nobody's supposed to get hurt, remember? I'll figure out something."

"You?"

Mom agreed to give me money for my *gi* and lessons. That night I dug around in the bathroom cupboard and found an old Ace bandage Dad used to use for his basketball knee. It would have to work.

The next day at school I had a new problem. The minute the bell rang, someone called out, "Good morning, kiddies!" in a Drog-like voice.

Gordy was the only one who laughed.

"Settle down, Parker," Mrs. Belcher said, frowning.

But it wasn't me. It wasn't Drog either.

During math, the same voice called out silly answers like, "There are two and a half centipedes in an inch" and "We reduce fractions because they're so fat."

"Parker?" Mrs. Belcher said. "Didn't we have an agreement?"

Wren turned around and waved at me behind that ventriloquism book.

"Cut it out, Wren," I said to her at recess.

"Well, I will if you will," she said. "You've been doing this ever since we found that puppet."

"No I haven't. And besides, I'd never do anything on purpose to get *you* in trouble."

She brushed a strand of hair out of her face. "I don't know," she said. "I don't know anymore what you would do."

At the dojo that day, I put on my *gi* for the first time. It fit loose in the arms and legs and smelled like pine soap.

"Pajamas!" Drog said.

I wrapped the Ace bandage around him mummy-style so he couldn't feel anything if we fell to the floor.

The girl with the orange belt noticed the bandage.

"What's that? Are you injured?"

"No."

"Well then, you should take that off. You can't do aikido with it on."

"I have to."

She put her hands on her hips. Why do girls do that, anyway?

"Why do you think we wear uniforms?" she asked. "You're not supposed to draw attention to yourself here."

"I can't help it."

"Well, let's see what Sensei says."

I waited on the mat with the others and tried to focus. *One-point one-point one-point.* Sensei had said Drog was welcome. *One-point.* He had said no one should get hurt. *One-point one-point.*

Sensei came in, and the girl nodded toward my bandaged hand. His expression stayed relaxed.

"Good," he said. "You've all been focusing on your center. I've asked Kelly here to demonstrate the basic roll technique. But first I want to do a demonstration of another kind. Parker, please step forward."

Uh-oh.

"Mike, please come and stand next to Parker."

Mike was in the beginner's group too, but a lot older.

"Parker, hold out your arm. Yes, straight out like that. Mike will push down on your arm as hard as he can, and you will do your best to keep him from moving it. Now."

The guy was over six feet tall, and his arm muscles had muscles. I tensed my arm and tried as hard as I could, but I couldn't resist for even a second.

"All right, Parker, please step outside with me. The rest of you go back to your one-point and think about ... possibilities."

Out on the sidewalk, Sensei said, "You're going to do this again in a few minutes, only this time Mike won't be able to move your arm at all."

"He won't?"

"Plant your feet firmly, about shoulder-width apart, one slightly ahead of the other. That's it. Now imagine that there is a big root extending down from each foot for about a mile."

Right away I felt steady.

"Put your arm out and see it reaching clear across town, even to the horizon."

My arm seemed to grow and grow.

"Now—most important—your one-point. We haven't talked yet about the enormous energy you have in there. When Mike pushes down on your arm, breathe out from your center and feel that energy flowing up and out through your arm to the horizon and out into space."

That sounded impossible, but Sensei was so sure that it made me want to try everything exactly the way he said.

"Don't think about Mike or the other students or me. Don't even look at anyone. Just focus on your one-point and all that energy flowing out through your arm."

We went back into the dojo. *One-point one-point one-point one-point one.* I got myself set and stuck out my arm.

"The other arm, this time," Sensei said.

Oh no.

Still looking at nobody, not even him, I stuck my Drog arm out and went back to concentrating, *one-point one-point,* thinking so hard about that energy that I barely noticed Mike come toward me. My arm was the longest tree limb in the world, and his hands were like birds that landed on it and then took off again.

The next thing I knew, people were clapping and Mike was staring at me.

"Awesome," he said.

"You may reset now, Parker," Sensei said. "Well everyone, what do you think happened here?"

Finally Mike said, "He's got something under that bandage."

Sensei laughed. "True, but that's not the answer. Do you think Parker suddenly developed his muscles and became super-strong? Could he do that in a few minutes?"

Everyone shook their heads.

"No. In aikido our strength doesn't come from size or muscles. It comes from our energy, our *ki.* I showed Parker how to focus his energy.

"By the way, Parker has learned something else important on his first day." He held up my bandaged Drog hand. "In aikido, we protect our opponent."

Kelly, the girl with the orange belt, helped us to get started with our rolls. After class she came over to congratulate me and say she was sorry. She even thanked me, which I couldn't figure out.

The other students wanted to know how I had managed to use the *ki* and how it felt. And what was under the bandage. When I showed them, they looked confused, but at least they didn't laugh.

"Do you have any idea how hot your hand got when you did that long-arm number?" Drog said as we stepped out into the street. "Most uncomfortable."

I smiled. "So why didn't you just imagine you were back in the desert with the emir?"

"Don't get smart with me," he said.

chapter eleven

Late one night, Mrs. Belcher got one of her Great Ideas. She decided our class should make a puppet theater and put on a puppet play. Everyone could tell she was doing this to keep me from becoming the class weirdo, but I appreciated it.

As soon as she brought up the puppet play idea in class, Big Boy boomed from the back of the room, "We could put it on for the kindergartners."

Kids stared at each other. It was easy to forget about Big Boy for days at a time because he didn't say much. Not in a loud voice, anyway. And when he did talk, he mostly said "man" and "cool." Nobody knew how old Big Boy was exactly. They say he had to repeat first grade, and then he spent two years in fifth. He barely fit his desk.

"That's a wonderful suggestion, Norbert," Mrs. Belcher said. She never called him Big Boy.

Everyone knew Big Boy picked kindergarten because his little sister was in that class, and he was crazy about her.

"As a matter of fact, the kindergarten is having its parents' night in just two weeks," Mrs. Belcher said. "Do you think we could be ready that soon?"

"Sure," we answered in a chorus.

"Since it's your idea, Norbert, maybe you'd like to pick the play?"

Way to go, Mrs. B. Take care of two oddballs at once.

"Um, how about The Three Little Pigs?" Big Boy said. "Lisa loves— I mean, I think that would be a good one for them."

"Excellent. The story and the lines are already familiar, and we don't have much time."

Mrs. Belcher was humming now. Her favorite part of any project is writing lists on the blackboard.

"Let's see, we'll need a stage and scenery and a script, and of course we'll need a mother pig, the three little pigs, and the wolf—that's five puppets. Hand puppets will be the simplest, I think. Parker you already have one . . ." *Very smooth, Mrs. Belcher.* ". . . so maybe you could just make a costume for it. Wren, will you help him?"

"Mmmmm," Wren said. I guessed that was supposed to be a yes.

Drog started muttering, so I put him up to my ear. "I am the big bad wolf, or I'm nobody," he said.

I raised my hand. "Can Drog be the wolf?"

"You have to try out, Parker," Big Boy said. "Let's hear you say the huff-and-puff part."

"Then I'll huff, and I'll PUFF, and I'll BLOOOOOOOOOOOOOOOOW your house down!" Drog said, adding a wicked cackle at the end. Everybody thought it was me.

Big Boy practically knocked over his seat laughing. Even Wren giggled. We were in.

Mrs. Belcher turns every project into an "Educational Opportunity." The kids making the theater had to go on the Internet and print out pictures of real puppet theaters from around the world. Most stood high off the ground, like towers, so that all the kids in a crowd could see. Wren's dad made the frame for ours, and the theater committee painted and decorated it and made a curtain you could pull open and closed.

The puppets had to be made from scratch with papier-mâché heads. Wren got to be the third little pig, and all I could do to help her was dunk the paper strips into the paste for the pig's head and hand them to her. She did help me sew the wolf costume, which was a good thing, because I sure couldn't do it one-handed.

Breathing the minty school-paste smell and working on something with Wren was beginning to make me feel almost like usual. She even came over to my house one day and brought some fake black fur she bought at the craft store. For eyes we found a couple of shiny red buttons in the spare room. The wolf costume turned out just about perfect.

"Wait," I said. "Drog has to be able to see out."

Wren gave me a dead-fish look.

"Make some eye holes under the buttons," I said.

"It's just a puppet, Parker. You're going to do all the seeing."

"Boy, if you're going to be doing all the seeing, we're in trouble," Drog said.

I ignored him. "He needs eye holes, Wren."

"Oh all right." She cut a couple of slits. "Do you have to be so weird?"

"Yeah," I said. "Looks like I do."

Mom was really happy when I told her about the play, and especially when Wren came over, so I told her I didn't think I needed to go back to see Dr. Mann.

"I'm definitely staying out of trouble," I said. I hoped that was true. How could I get into any more trouble than I was in already?

"That's good, Parker," Mom said, "but I promised the school."

Dr. Mann liked hearing about the play, especially since Drog was part of it. But mostly he asked a lot about Dad, his work, what I remembered about living with him, things like that. Drog refused to say anything during our appointment. He wouldn't even put words in my mouth.

———

Three days to the puppet performance and everything was coming together on schedule. The scenery committee painted the pigs' houses of sticks and stones and bricks on flats to hold up behind the stage. Big Boy, who got to be the director, decided that we needed sound effects, so he took a tambourine from the music closet and brought in some balloons to blow up.

He rattled the tambourine each time the wolf huffed and puffed, and when he blew, Big Boy let the air out of one of the balloons. It sounded more like a fart, actually, but Big Boy glared around the room, daring anyone to laugh.

Rehearsals went okay. Drog cooperated, saying his lines over and over on cue, and everybody thought I was a good actor. But after school the day before our performance, Drog said to me, "The play is boring. Tell Mrs. Burper I'm not doing it."

I groaned. Just when I was starting to feel half-normal, Drog might clam up completely during the play and mess me up again.

"What do you mean Drog?" I said. "You're the wolf! You've got the best part. And nobody else can do it now, it's too late."

"I have decided. Drog doesn't do kiddie plays."

I didn't argue with him, just ignored him and hoped he'd change his mind. He had to. But the next day in rehearsal I had to cover for him.

"Little Pig, Little Pig, let me come in," I said. It didn't sound one-tenth as wolfly as Drog. Big Boy stopped the rehearsal.

"C'mon, man, do it like you did yesterday. You sound like a wimp."

I didn't get much better, and by the end everybody was mad at me.

Mrs. Belcher called us into a circle. "You know, an old tradition in the theater says bad dress rehearsal, great performance. Everyone go home now, and don't worry. You're doing a good thing for the kindergartners, and you're going to be fine."

"Whoooooooeeeee, did you ever sound pathetic!" Drog said on the way home. "You wouldn't know a wolf from a wiener dog, ha-ha!"

"Drog," I said, trying to sound much calmer than I felt, "you have to do the play. Because if you don't, it'll be really embarrassing. There could be forty or fifty people there. Not just kids, but adults, too—teachers and parents."

"My public."

"Yes."

"My big chance."

"Yes."

"And only Drog can do the role."

"Right!"

"Very well, then. This once."

Big Boy's little sister, Lisa, sat cross-legged down front, jabbering with her class, while the adults took folding chairs or stood in the back. Mrs. Belcher introduced the cast and crew and the kids in our class who worked on the play, which was everybody. When she announced that Big Boy—er, Norbert—was the director, Lisa grinned like a cat who'd caught a bird.

The play started out better than it ever did in the classroom. Big Boy's sound effects actually worked okay. Drog hammed it up a bit with the first two pigs, but by Drog standards, he was behaving himself. Then Wren came on with the third pig, the one who's supposed to outsmart the wolf. The cooking pot waited for the wolf to climb down the chimney.

When Wren got to the "Not by the hair of my chinny chin chin" part, Drog said, "Oh, come on, Little Pork Chop, it's me, Gunga Din."

A few giggles bubbled through the audience, and one of the fathers laughed out loud.

"Not by the hair of my chinny chin *chin*," Wren said.

"It's Publisher's Sweepstakes," Drog answered. "Think what you'll win."

Wren pinched my arm. Hard.

"Shut *up*, Drog," I said.

There was no stopping him. He squeezed my hand so suddenly and hard that I batted the brick house aside and knocked Wren's pig into the cooking pot. Then he said, "Oh, I do love a good pork ragout, don't you?"

I looked at Wren. Half of her was mad, and that half was trying hard to keep the other half from laughing.

The crowd howled, but everyone behind the stage was shoving and punching me.

Drog called out to the kindergartners, "Have I been a bad, bad wolf?"

"Yes!" they cheered.

Wren pulled the curtain, but Drog peeked out again.

"Oh, shall I be good then?"

"Nooooooooooooo!"

"Shall I be horribly horrible?"

"Yeeeeeessssss!"

"Well," he snickered, "wait till you see what I do to Red Riding Hood—and her grandmamma too."

"No! No!" Big Boy's sister Lisa wailed, but almost everybody else laughed.

Somebody pulled my Drog hand back in while Wren yanked the curtain closed again. The audience clapped and hollered.

"Just listen to that applause," Drog said. "I was magnifico!"

Wren let her mad half win. "I hope you're proud of yourself, Parker," she fumed. "You've just ruined the play."

But I only half-listened, because a red-faced Big Boy was heading toward us right then with his fists balled up, about to pop.

"Drog," I said, "we gotta get out of here."

chapter twelve

I bolted out the gym door and ducked out of sight on one side of the concrete steps. Big Boy ran down the steps and looked both ways, clenching and unclenching his hands. Then he took off toward the playground.

As soon as his back was turned, I tiptoe-dashed for the Fremont Street entrance. The floodlight didn't reach to that end of the schoolyard, and the streetlight made a deep shadow of the steps. Perfect. I crouched down and got ready to wait a while.

Not too long, I hoped, because I forgot my jacket inside. The ground, the wall, and the concrete steps all felt super cold. My teeth knocked together and the air smelled like snow.

"Well," Drog said. "I practically had those little monsters wetting their pants, didn't I, Boy?"

Actually, it was pretty funny when I thought about it. I pictured Wren with her hands on her hips, bawling me out, and I laughed a shivery laugh out loud. I couldn't help it. I didn't hear Big Boy come up behind me.

"There you are!"

He must have run all the way around the school. No point in hiding any more. I stood up.

"Give me that crazy puppet, man. I'm throwing it in the trash can!"

"Aaaaeeeeeeeeeeeee!" screamed Drog.

"No! Wait! You don't understand," I said.

"Understand? I understand you wrecked my play!"

"I'm sorry about the play, Big Boy, but—"

"Give me that thing!"

I couldn't believe how fast he tackled me, grabbed Drog by the head, and tried to rip him off my hand.

For a second I thought, ALL RIGHT! HE CAN DO THIS! But only the wolf costume came off. Drog held on.

"Let . . . go . . . you!" Big Boy grunted at me.

"Can't," I panted.

Big Boy pinned my two wrists to the ground with one hand, and with the other he reached into his pocket and pulled out something shiny. A cigarette lighter!

"Jeez, Big Boy, I didn't know you smoked," cracked Drog.

Big Boy's grip tightened. "Shut up, Parker!"

"Shut UP, Drog," I said.

Big Boy flicked the lighter, trying to get it to catch. "You gonna take this thing off or not? 'Cause I'm torchin' it either way!"

"Murder! Murder!" Drog screamed.

I imagined my whole hand on fire, like picking up a dozen lit sparklers from the wrong end. Even I didn't want to get rid of Drog that bad. *Think of something. Anything.*

"Over, here, Dad!" I yelled over Big Boy's shoulder. "Great! You're just in time!"

Big Boy fell for it. He turned to look behind him, and his grip loosened just enough that I could jerk my hands free, roll to the side, get up, and run like crazy for home.

"Parker!" Mom said. "I thought you were going to call me when you were ready."

"Oh, uh, I decided to walk."

"In your T-shirt? You must be frozen! Where in the world is your jacket?"

"Sorry. I left it at school."

She made me put on a sweatshirt and drove me back to the gym. The custodian was just locking up, and he had my jacket propped on the handle of his push broom. If he had seen what happened at the play, he didn't say anything.

"I'm getting plenty worried about you, Parker," Mom said on the drive home.

I could see it. The frown lines between her eyebrows had deepened to valleys, and I felt like a steaming pile of dog poop. With Dad gone, I should be trying to avoid getting her upset instead of making more trouble. If only I could just . . . take care of all this.

Even with my sweatshirt and my jacket on, I was shaking, but I tried not to let it show.

"I'm okay, Mom," I said. "Trust me."

I went straight upstairs and took a hot shower, holding Drog up out of the stream of water.

I probably should have felt good about fooling Big Boy, but I just felt tired. Tired of Drog. Tired of trouble and confusion. Tired of myself. How pathetic was that, calling to Dad for help, even if the trick worked?

"The thing is, Boy," Drog said as I toweled off, "never let them know you're afraid."

"Listen, Drog, I got us out of that one, but you got us into it in the first place. From now on will you just keep your big mouth shut? Or at least speak for yourself, not me!"

"Ungrateful boy. I'm just showing you what life's all about."

"Huh! How would you know? You're nothing but a talking head!"

That shut him up for the rest of the night.

I was pretty sure I knew what was waiting for me when I got to school the next day. I was wrong. Big Boy was nowhere on the playground.

He was in the classroom, sitting in my seat. The minute I came in, kids stopped talking or fooling around to watch. With his thumb, Big Boy pointed to his old seat in the back with my stuff piled on it. I went.

I fumbled in my book bag, putting things away in the desk one by one to give everybody time to get bored with snickering or giving me stink-eye. Then I looked up. "Room 202 is a Drog-free Zone!" the blackboard exclaimed, and "Just Say No to Drogs." Wren's handwriting.

Mrs. Belcher came in, put her papers down, and stood in front of her desk, her signal for us to pay attention.

"Parker, what are you doing back there?"

"Um, Big Boy and I traded seats."

She looked at me, then Big Boy, then me. "Well, all right, then. I see you've worked it out. Wren, please erase the board."

Wren looked past me on the way back to her desk.

Mrs. Belcher set her papers aside. "Now about the play last night."

I slid down in my seat.

"It didn't go at all the way we rehearsed it," she said. Why was she smiling? "But sometimes unplanned things turn out best in the end. If our goal was to entertain the kindergarteners and their parents, I would have to say we succeeded, wouldn't you?"

Nods all around, but Big Boy folded his arms, and Wren tried to disappear me with a laser look.

Mrs. Belcher went on. "Everyone worked hard on the play, and we should be proud," she said, "but I think we owe special thanks to Parker—or, I should say, to Drog—for our success. Take a bow, Drog."

She and the kids clapped and turned toward me.

Oh no. I pulled him out and held him up. The class hooted and clapped even louder. Not that Drog needed any encouragement.

"My fans," he said. "Congratulations on casting me as the wolf for our first production. We were boffo last night, at least I was, and I wish to thank—actually, why should I thank anyone but myself? And who is this Parker person of whom you speak? A stagehand, perhaps? Shall I blow his house down?"

I jammed him into my pocket.

Mrs. Belcher burst out laughing and couldn't stop. The class did too—all but two, who just got madder.

"Oh, Parker, you're so funny," the girl in front of me said. "How do you *do* that?"

I spoke up so everybody could hear me. "I *don't* do it. It's like Drog says, I'm just a stagehand."

But nobody got what I was trying to say.

Was that going to be my life now? Sitting in the back and having everyone misunderstand for different reasons?

At recess Wren came over to me, linking elbows with two other girls. "We heard you beat up Big Boy after you ruined his play," she said. "How could you do that?"

If it had been anyone but Wren, I would have laughed.

"I couldn't. I didn't. I got away, that's all."

"Nobody believes you anymore, *amigo*. And Drog is a drag."

"I guess that just about sums it up," I said.

It killed me the way she said "amigo" and meant the opposite. She looked so disgusted as she turned away. Couldn't she understand what that was like, to have nobody believe you?

I realized walking home that Drog hadn't said a word all day, at least not to me.

I held him up to my face. "Drog, can you tell me how I manage to get everyone who matters mad at me?"

"Well, I wouldn't know, would I?" he sniffed. "I'm nothing but a talking head."

So that was it. For a minute I actually felt bad and almost apologized, but I stopped just in time. Why should I apologize to Drog? About anything? After all the things he'd said to me, all the ways he was ruining my life, how could my one little talking-head insult bother him so much?

I didn't have to worry. By the time we got home and up to my room, he was yakking again.

"For our next production, you and I will write the script," he said. "Or rather I will dictate and you will write it down. How about 'A Day at the Camel Races'? Or 'Little

Dumber Boy Does Christmas'? Or 'Exorcist, the Musical'? I also sing, you know. A sonorous baritone."

I reached for Wren's geode on the shelf over my desk and turned its crystals to the wall. It looked too much like an eye.

The next day, Mrs. Belcher asked if I could stay a few minutes after school. I probably wasn't in any more trouble, or she wouldn't ask; she'd tell me to stay.

It turned out she wanted me to watch a video she had picked up about these supposedly famous puppets called Punch and Judy.

"I thought you might like to know that yours is not the only badly behaved puppet in the world," she said.

The video combined clips from old-time Punch and Judy shows at county fairs all over England and America and in some other countries, too. The puppet master would carry his theater on his back and set up in any park or town square, and the people, mostly children, would gather around to watch.

I couldn't get over how totally mean the Punch character was. Even when he did something wrong, he just made fun of anyone who complained. Or hit them over the head. He and his wife Judy argued all the time and beat on each other. And the audience loved it.

"I never heard of Punch and Judy before," I told Mrs. Belcher.

"Well, a lot of people haven't these days. After hundreds of years, the tradition is dying out."

"I didn't think Punch was funny. Did you?"

"Not really, but times have changed. For one thing, people are more worried about violence right now than they have been in the past."

"I sure am," I said. I thought of Big Boy and his lighter.

Mrs. Belcher put the video back in its envelope and gave it to me to borrow.

Drog was awfully quiet all the way home. But when I started to replay the video, he cried out, "No! No! Put me in your pocket! Stick your hand in the trash can!"

"Drog! What's the matter with you?"

"Do as I say!"

"No. Not until you tell me why."

"Drog hates Punch!"

"How come? Because he's so nasty?"

"Yes! Yes! Would Drog beat people to death for no good reason? Would Drog throw a baby out the window?"

"I—"

"Exactly! Don't you see, Boy? Punch is ten times worse than Drog can ever hope to be. And people love him. Oh, I wish I'd never seen the Punch and Judy show!"

So that was it. "Drog! You're jealous of Punch!"

"Jealous? Ha! Drog is never jealous."

"Anyway, we don't have to watch that video again. I'll take it back to Mrs. Belcher tomorrow."

"Well, all right then," he said.

As we climbed into bed that night, I said to him, "Drog, have you ever thought . . . maybe you don't have to be so bad?"

"Oh, please. What else would I be? If Drog isn't wicked, he's nothing."

He started to snore, and I tried to sleep too, but I lay there wondering, is it some people's nature to be bad like Drog said? What about Big Boy? He'd get in huge trouble if I told anybody he almost set my hand on fire. That was serious stuff. But he wasn't bad, just mad, and I couldn't blame him.

Only why did Drog feel he had to be bad? It didn't make any sense. Where did he come from that bad was good? Or at least not bad?

chapter thirteen

Drog kept bugging me about aikido, especially the night Sensei had some of the advanced students show us how to use the bamboo sword and defend against a multiple-sword attack.

"That's it? That's the best they can do?" Drog said after practice. "They wouldn't survive in a mouse fight. Oh, if you could only have been with me at Shaolin Temple. You had to stand in the snow for three days and nights without blinking an eye just to get admitted to that place."

"You were at the Shaolin Temple?"

"Was I at Shaolin? You've heard of Bruce Lee?"

"Sure!"

"Well, who do you think watched Bruce go through his entire training with the monks? Believe me, those Shaolin fellows didn't *practice*, they fought for keeps. With their fists and feet and with the most treacherous weapons."

"Aikido uses weapons."

"Oh, please. Broomsticks, wooden knives."

"People get injured."

"Yes, but how? Falling down? A Shaolin monk would be ashamed to fall down. Aikido is for losers!"

Before practice the next day I said to Drog, "Falling isn't that easy, you know. Want to try it?"

"What do you mean?"

"I mean, you don't really know what it's like because I wear this Ace bandage. But I'm tired of wearing it. Now that I'm getting better at falling, why don't I just practice without it?"

"You're going to try to hurt me."

"I'm going to try *not* to. This is aikido, remember? Scared?"

"Drog is never scared."

Sensei took one look at my unwrapped hand and paired me with himself. We spent the hour adjusting my moves so that I could still use my Drog hand without twisting or hitting Drog's head. I missed a couple of times and told Drog I was sorry, but he ignored me.

"We did it, Drog," I said as we finished up.

"I don't plan to get used to this," he grumbled.

"Okay Drog," I said to him when we got home, "Help me write a story for Mrs. Belcher. It's supposed to be a true story. So what'll I write? How about your ruby yacht one?"

"No! That's . . . top secret!"

"Top secret? How come?"

He sniffed. "I'm not at liberty to say."

"Well, what then? You're full of stories."

"I'm . . . not inspired at the moment."

"Maybe I should tell the true story of a boy who got a puppet stuck to his hand."

"Ha! You'd get it all wrong."

I put Drog away in my pocket, took out my notebook, and just started writing. The story that spilled out on the paper was about a boy whose father took him up in a glider plane. The height scared him at first, but his dad was all excited and not worried at all, so pretty soon the boy got used to being up in the air.

His dad pointed out things on the ground: the grain silos gleaming like silver buttons from up there, the trains getting switched around in the railroad yards, the green-and-tan patchwork patterns the fields of corn and soybeans made. Except for the two of them talking, everything was quiet. Whenever the wings caught drafts of air, the plane rose a little. *This must be what a bird feels*, the boy thought.

"Uh-oh," his dad said, pointing to a tall gray cloud east of town. Just below it was a blur of rain, and they could smell and taste wet dust in the air. He guided the plane down and down, and it touched the ground without a bounce. Then the rain hit in huge, bursting drops. By the time the dad and the boy ran to the hangar, their drenched clothes stuck to them and they were laughing. They drove to a diner in the rain and slurped sweet hot chocolate.

I asked Mom, but she couldn't remember that time. She said Dad hadn't gone soaring in years and I would have been too little to go along. But it was a good story. I was pretty sure it was true.

I hoped so, because Mrs. Belcher wanted the whole class to hear it. While I was reading, I glanced sideways. Big Boy was listening to every word, but when I finished and looked up from the paper at him, he looked away.

Wren came up to me after school and just stood in front of me like she wanted to tell me something but it might take her all day to get it out. I wanted to say, "I get it. You're supposed to be a door." But that sounded Drog-like and she'd probably take it the wrong way, so I waited her out.

"That boy was you, wasn't it?" she finally said. "You and your dad."

I nodded. Wren. The one person who could understand about my dad and me.

"Well, I don't think I like you very much right now," she said, tossing her braid back over her shoulder. "But I liked your story. I liked it a lot."

I didn't know whether to say thanks to that or not, so I kind of changed the subject. "I was going to tell one Drog told me. About this boat covered with rubies, the Ruby Yacht of Omar Khayyam. It was practically one of the wonders of the world once, he said, but it disappeared."

Wren shifted the weight of her backpack for the walk home. "His story couldn't have been as good as yours."

"How's your friend doing?" Sensei asked before practice.

"My friend? Oh, you mean Drog. Bossy as ever." Drog squeezed. "He doesn't like aikido practice. Makes fun of me."

"But you come anyway."

I nodded.

"Good. Respect him, Parker. All right, everybody, approach the mat."

That didn't make sense. How could anybody respect Drog? Especially me, his prisoner? If anything, Drog needed to respect me.

We practiced our throws for a while. Then Sensei said, "Have you ever known people who seem to have eyes in the back of their heads?"

Some of us nodded.

"Well, you may not think so now, but you can learn that. Not to see, exactly, but to sense what's happening around you, even with your eyes closed or your back turned. Even if the movement is silent. Because everyone puts out energy. Good energy. Bad energy. Nervous energy. Gentle energy.

"When you center yourself, you can begin to sense what kind of energy is coming from the people around you. First the ones you see, and then those who approach you from behind. You not only *can* do this, you *must*, if you really want to do aikido. Beginning today, ask yourself what kind of energy is in each person you meet. Awareness. It's all practice."

On the way out, I tried to check out the storage closet without being noticed. But Sensei said, "Looking for something?"

"Do you have any really big *gi*?"

He laughed. "We have all sizes."

He showed me a pair with pants that I could have climbed into one leg of. "Do you have someone in mind?"

"Maybe."

"Boy, you'd better not be thinking what I think you're thinking," Drog said.

Mom was on the phone when I got home.

"Well, you'll be happy to hear he's taken up a sport, Brian, a martial arts class. . . . No, not karate. It's called aikido. . . . Oh, he's getting a few bruises, but he seems to like it. . . . No. No, he's still got it on. . . . It's not a doll Brian, it's a puppet. . . . I'm doing everything I can, believe— What's that supposed to mean? . . . Of course, here he is now. Hold on. Parker?"

One-point one-point. "Hello, Dad."

"Hi, Son. Your mother tells me you're taking martial arts lessons. That's great."

"Uh-huh."

"So what do they teach you?

"Um. How to fight so nobody gets hurt."

"Oh, you pull your punches?"

"No, we learn how to fall."

"Oh? Well, that . . . puppet of yours must be taking a beating."

"No, he isn't. I protect him."

"Wow, Parker. You're really into this, aren't you?"

"You mean aikido?"

"I mean—I'm glad that you're taking these lessons."

What kind of energy was coming from Dad? I didn't know. Maybe you couldn't tell over the phone.

chapter fourteen

Actually, my seat in the back of the room was a good place to practice figuring out people's energy. I held my book up and made little drawings of people behind it, just a few scribbly lines, and that helped me get a feeling about them.

Mrs. Belcher's name didn't fit her, I decided. In my drawing she looked sort of like a friendly deer: big, but quick and smart with large eyes. She could be called Mrs. Deerfield. Can't adults change their names if they want? Wouldn't you do that if your name was Belcher? Especially if you were a teacher? She had a different look sometimes when she was mad. I drew that one, too, from memory—a porcupine.

And Wren? Wren was hard. I'd drawn her lots of times—the way she keeps her back perfectly straight even when she's sitting cross-legged, the way she looks far off or chews on the end of her braid when she's thinking. But Wren was always Wren, and everything she did and said just seemed like her. I never wondered why before, never tried to figure her out.

Okay, if Wren was an animal, what kind of animal would she be? Well, she loves dogs. Maybe a terrier, because they're really active and determined and nervous. But she's like that mostly about little things like tests and assignments, and mostly at school. In big things, she's calm and strong, and she can figure things out, even in emergencies. She's even talked about being a rescue worker someday. So make her a huge Newfoundland who dashes into the ocean and saves people without even being told to.

Right. Wren wouldn't even help rescue her own best friend. I gave up trying to draw her. Too much mad energy getting in the way.

For Big Boy I drew a bear in boy's clothes. A tame bear with a kind of sad expression, like he didn't expect much anymore, but he wished people would just treat him like a bear and not make him wear those stupid pants.

I studied the drawing for a while and decided I didn't like having Big Boy be mad at me, so I got up my nerve and walked up to him at recess.

"Norbert, can I talk to you about something?"

He turned and glared at me.

I swallowed. "I . . . I don't blame you for being mad about Drog and the play, but the thing is, I can't control him."

"Huh. I don't believe you."

I took my Drog hand out of my pocket and looked at it. "Yeah. If I wasn't me, I probably wouldn't believe me either."

"So?" He started to turn away.

"So . . . why don't you come with me tonight to my aikido class?" I said it fast.

"I knew it!" Drog said.

Big Boy turned back. "Aikido? What's that?"

"It's a kind of martial arts."

"Martial arts? That's fighting, right? You get to fight?"

"What? Yeah, you get to fight. But without getting mad, you know? You stay cool."

"Cool, huh? I get to fight you?"

"You get to fight everybody."

He drew in the dirt with the toe of his shoe and didn't say anything or a while. I didn't say anything either, just waited.

"Well. Maybe I will."

"Okay, that's great, Norbert."

He wrinkled his nose. "Call me Big Boy, man. Sounds better than Norbert."

"Okay, Big Boy. I'll call you later."

"That does it! You are out of your mop," Drog said on the way home.

Mom got off early from work so she could drive us. I knew she was glad I was doing something with somebody in my class, but except for smiling too much, she played it cool.

As we got out of the car, she said, "I'll pick you boys up at 6:30, okay?" *Good, Mom, you didn't invite Big Boy for supper or anything.*

"It's good that we have a new student tonight," Sensei said, "because I've brought something that will help us review and will also show . . . Big Boy is it?" Big Boy nodded. ". . . what aikido is about."

He passed out some small tubes woven out of colored straw.

"Everybody take one of these Chinese finger puzzles, and push your index fingers into each end."

I only had one index finger free, so I just did one end.

"All right now, get your fingers out."

I braced the other end of the puzzle between my knees. But the more I pulled, the tighter the thing got.

Everybody else was trapped, too.

"Ow!"

"I can't!"

Some kids got red in the face, and one boy looked worried, like he might never get his fingers out. I pictured myself with a puppet stuck on one hand and a finger trap stuck on the other for the rest of my life.

Sensei clapped his hands, and we all jumped.

"What is the first step in a conflict?" he boomed.

"Find your one-point!" we answered in a chorus.

"Then?"

"Blend with the attacker!"

"Then?"

"Enter and turn the attack to the side!"

"Yes," he said, in a quiet voice this time. "Now you can solve the finger puzzle."

Everyone stopped pulling and pushed inward instead. Right away the weave loosened. We turned our fingers sideways, and they came out. Easy.

"Cool," Big Boy said.

Sensei raised his eyebrows at me, smiled and nodded, then stepped onto the mat. What did that look mean? Oh! Maybe he was showing me one way I hadn't tried yet to get Drog off.

Good idea. Instead of pulling, I pushed my hand *into* Drog then turned it, just like you do to open a medicine bottle. But he stayed as stuck as ever.

"C'mon baby, let's do the Twist," he cracked.

Sensei paired himself with Big Boy, and I watched them whenever I got a chance. I thought Big Boy would have trouble because he had so far to fall, but he did great. It was fun to watch him fall and roll. Seeing him with Sensei made me realize that he really was older than us sixth-graders. It must be hard for him to spend all day, every day, with younger kids.

"Some fools are bigger than others," Drog said.

But I knew Big Boy was going to get his *gi*, and I was glad.

Dad came to Ferrisburg on Saturday. I got only about a half-hour's notice from Mom.

"Why's he coming?" I said.

"To see you, he says." She reached for her coat. "It'll just be the two of you. I'm going over to Nicole's."

This had to be about Drog. "Did he sound mad or anything?"

"Nope."

I was glad I didn't have too much time to think about it, because seeing Dad was sure to be a disaster. Of course he would want to hear Drog talk, and of course Drog would pull his silent act like he did with Wren, which would just prove I was a dumb problem kid who made things up.

My best hope, my only plan, was to keep Drog in my pocket the whole time and refuse to take him out.

Mom hugged me just before she left. "Good luck," she said. "Try to give your dad a chance, now."

Me give him a chance? But I nodded, and then she was gone.

The minutes raced toward two o'clock, even when I finally remembered my one-point. The doorbell rang, and I jumped. For a minute I thought, "who's that?"

chapter fifteen

Dad. Ringing the bell of a house that used to be his house, even though he knew I was the only one inside. I breathed out, reminded myself to keep Drog put away, tried one more one-point, and opened the door.

"Hi, Parker," Dad said, looking straight into my eyes.

I couldn't answer. I couldn't remember the last time he'd looked right at me at me like that.

I wasn't expecting him to be dressed like he was, either—faded jeans and hooded sweatshirt instead of a dress shirt and pants. I looked down at his feet—green socks and leather moccasins, newer ones like the scuffed old pair in the back of the hall closet. He was dressed to hang out.

He smiled. "Well. Okay if I come in, Parker?"

I said something that sounded like "'k," and he came

in and sat down on the couch as if he lived here. I almost expected him to put his feet up on the magazine table.

He started talking about this wild-looking scarecrow he had seen in a cornfield on the way over from Moline and about a huge flock of migrating red-winged blackbirds that swooped down and stuck all over it. He asked me what I did for Halloween. I relaxed a little and tried to make the conversation go on, being careful not to mention Mom or Wren. Or Drog. Postponing, postponing.

Finally Dad said, "So, Parker, How about letting me see this puppet everybody's been talking about?"

One-point. One-point. "You don't really want to meet him, Dad."

"Sure I do. That's one reason I'm here. The other reason is, I wanted to see you."

I wanted to see you. I let that sink in.

"Dad, I don't think . . . I mean, I need to keep him put away."

He didn't argue, just stood up and said, "C'mon. Let's go for a ride."

I grabbed my jacket and followed him out. When I opened the car door it hit me, the smell of him in the car, the brown smell. That sounds awful, but I mean the smell of warm coffee and leather and cloves and cinnamon—from his shaving lotion, I guess—all mixed together. The memories in that smell surprised me, made me feel like a little kid again, and I wished I could cry for myself.

Dad drove north on Prairie for a few blocks, humming, then he signaled left and said, "Mind if we check out my old family place out on Maple? I haven't been by there in years."

"Okay," I said. I couldn't get over how easy he was being with me, like we were a couple of good friends getting together on a Saturday. Hope crept up on me and filled my chest. Maybe I could talk to Dad after all. Get him to believe me and understand. He was taking his time with me. We had all afternoon. Maybe there was enough time.

He pulled up in front of a small green house with one of those white plastic fences around it that you order from a catalog and set down in your yard.

"I sure had some good times growing up here," he said, "even though we didn't have much. Of course the place was different then. Wonder why the new owners painted it green? Makes it look even smaller." He turned to me, faking a pout-face, and said, "Parker, this house is supposed to be *yellow*!"

I tried to imagine it yellow. I tried to imagine Dad as a kid.

"And our fence was wood. Of course it needed to be fixed and painted all the time. My job. They've solved that problem, all right. This one looks like it will last past the end of the world."

"It's kind of ugly," I said.

Dad laughed. "You got that right. Oh no, they've ripped out the Concord grapevine now. That was the one thing we did have that was special. See that oak tree over there? Dad hung a tire swing from it for me, and I used to come home from school, pick a big bunch of grapes to eat, and swing as high as I could, spitting out the skins."

There was only a clothesline where he pointed now.

"Oh well," Dad said. "It's their house. They can do what they want with it."

He started up the engine again, and we drove to the to the baseball park and got out. The grass was all brown and matted, but we could make out the diamond. Dad jogged over to the batter's box and said, "Pitch me one of those killer high slow ones that'll drop right on me." I pretended to pitch him a ball, not so easy with one hand in my pocket, and he swung.

"Strike one!" he yelled, and crouched down again. He tapped home base with his pretend bat and said, "Now put one right where I want it." I pitched it again and he swung and ran for first. But I made it a fly ball, caught it one-handed. Would he be mad? No, he grinned.

"Got me," he said.

His breathing slowed down, and then he said, suddenly, "About this puppet, Parker. Do you really think you've got a big psychological problem here that needs a doctor?"

I looked down and shook my head.

"Well, I'm glad, because neither do I. It seems like you're just stuck and can't find your way out of this. I'd like to help you get unstuck. How does that sound?"

"Good," I said. "That sounds good." At last.

He put his arm around my shoulder and led me over to a picnic table. We sat on the same side, facing out toward the field.

"Do you know that when I was about your age, I got chosen to be the world's youngest astronaut?" Dad said.

"You didn't!"

"You're right, I didn't, but everybody I knew thought I did."

"How could you be an astronaut? You were just a kid!"

"Well, that didn't stop me, as you'll see in a minute. You comfortable? This could take a while."

"I'm good," I said. I wouldn't have moved for anything.

chapter sixteen

"I didn't just love math and science in school," Dad said. "I also loved Julie Anderson who sat in front of me in sixth grade. I can still picture her shiny hair hanging down almost over the top of my desk. Julie's smile ended in a dimple on one side, and she wore furry pink sweaters and smelled like bath soap.

She was everybody's girlfriend—they wished—but I had one particular rival for her attention named Brad. He was way better-looking than me, so I had to hope Julie liked smart boys and didn't listen to Brad when he called me a nerd. She did seem pretty impressed when the solar-powered model car I built took first in the district science fair. These days, you can just order one online, but not then.

"So off I went one weekend to the Museum of Science and Industry in Chicago for the state-level competition, and when I came back to school the following Monday, showing off my Honorable Mention ribbon, I found out that Brad had asked Julie to the movies on Saturday, just the two of them. I didn't like the way she kept smiling at him that day. I had to do something, fast, right? So I asked her if I could talk to her alone because I had something important to tell her, something private."

"How much you liked her?"

"Well that would have been the simple truth, wouldn't it? But what if she'd said thanks, but she liked Brad now? I'd have died."

"So what did you say?"

Dad chuckled then. "I can't believe I'm telling you this . . ."

I couldn't either, but I hoped it was going to be a very long story.

"Don't ask me where this came from, Parker, but I told Julie that my trip to Chicago wasn't really about the science fair at all. That was a cover so I could have a top-secret interview with NASA. They were planning to send three young boys on an expedition to Mars. I was accepted, so I would be going into training at the NASA academy that summer, and the launch would be about nine months later. We'd be twelve years old at liftoff. I told her she had to swear to secrecy— nobody was supposed to know about it until it happened, because we had to surprise the Russians."

"But Dad, why would they send boys?"

"Of course Julie asked me the same thing. I had all her attention by then, and those pretty eyes of hers got bigger and bigger, so my story did too.

"Mars is a lot farther from Earth than the moon, I explained, and even with the new superfast rocket they were working on that very moment, getting there and back would take a lot more time than people had ever spent out in space. Most experienced astronauts were too old to endure the exposure, but scientists thought young boys could take it. The astronauts would communicate with us from Earth, telling us what to do, but we'd be the ones up there doing it. 'But Brian, they don't actually know you can take it, do they?' Julie said. 'It could be dangerous!' I tell you, Parker, Julie was mine!"

"You mean she actually believed all that stuff?"

"She sure did. Heck, I got so wound up inventing it that I half-believed it myself. But the other half of me realized I was going to need a way out when all of this didn't happen, especially if I wanted to spend the summer going to movies with Julie. So I said of course it really all depended on NASA staying on schedule to develop that high-speed rocket and the special Mars suits for us. If they got too far behind, they'd have to choose three other boys. We'd be too old."

"Geez, Dad. But you said everybody thought you were going. Did Julie tell them?"

"Not right away. She asked me why I had told her about all this if it was supposed to be top secret. I said, because when I go off to the Space Academy this summer, no one will know where I am, and I want you to know. She got tears in her eyes then and said it would be our secret. I was in heaven. Of course, it wasn't so heavenly having to pretend to be getting in perfect shape for the training, because I had to pass up french fries and sloppy joes in the cafeteria and settle for carrot sticks and skim milk. Julie was there to remind me.

"Meanwhile, of course, Brad was ready to explode watching Julie hang around me all the time. One day I guess he'd seen about enough of her Brian worship, and he found an excuse to tackle me on the playground.

"He couldn't get in a punch though, because Julie came over and pulled his hair and said, 'Don't you dare hurt Brian, Brad. He's special. He's not even going to seventh grade with us next year, he's going to Mars!'

"Suddenly twelve kids were all ears, and I had to swear them to silence. You can probably guess how well that worked. Brad went straight to my sister and asked her if it was true, and she said no, all I had done was go to the fair and the museum and she had been with me the whole time. And Brad told Julie. This time Julie said she wanted to talk to me alone."

I drew my finger across my throat. "So you had to admit to her that you lied, right?" I said.

"You'd think so, wouldn't you? But no! I didn't!"

Dad burst out laughing then, and it was catching. When he could talk again he said, "Of course my sister would deny it, I told her. She had to try to stop the secret from spreading and getting us into trouble with the government. My sister was really mad at me for breaching security, I said. Then Julie started crying and saying it was all her fault for not keeping quiet, and I felt like a cockroach in a manure pile.

"Meanwhile my sister threatened to tell Mom and Dad. Unless of course I gave her half my allowance and took out the trash until kingdom come. But at least Julie was still my girlfriend. For about a day."

"How'd she find out?"

"I had to tell her myself. Somehow my parents got wind of it, and I got the I'm-so-disappointed-in-you lecture of all time from Mom. Dad informed me that I would not be breathing the air, much less eating at home until I came clean with Julie and apologized to her and to everybody who had believed me.

"So I went to her house and stood there until she came out. She just cried and said 'No, no' when I told her and asked me how I could do that to her. What was I going to say, because I liked her so much?

"The next day I had real pains in my stomach and didn't want to go to school, but Mom wasn't buying it. At least I didn't have to give my sister any of my allowance and I could eat all the french fries I wanted, but I had lost Julie, who still sat in front of me but didn't turn around anymore."

"I bet Brad was happy."

"Not really. Turned out, she didn't want to have anything more to do with him, either. You know, the only thing he ever said to me about it all was, 'Well, genius. How smart was that?' He had a point."

"Were the other kids all mad at you?"

"Oh sure. Nobody likes to be fooled. But pretty soon they realized they had something big on me they could tease me about for the rest of our lives. They called me Space Cadet way into high school.

"But it wasn't a complete disaster, really. I finally figured out that everyone loves having a great story to hold over some-body they know. Even I thought it was funny after a while."

Space Cadet. I smiled and shook my head.

Dad crossed one leg over the other knee and retied his moc-casin, then leaned back, his arm around my shoulder again.

"It could be like that for you, Parker. With this puppet business. If you let me, I'd like to figure out with you how this all happened. But for now my advice to you is, just tell the whole truth, quick and simple, and get it over with, like ripping off a Band-Aid. People like you. They always have. And they'll forgive you. It won't be so bad, I promise."

I leaned into him. "I wish I could do that, Dad."

"You can."

"No I can't, I mean, not the way you think."

He pointed to my pocket. "How about bringing that puppet out now, so I can see it?"

How could I say no? I pulled Drog out.

"Wow," Dad said, still relaxed and friendly. "That sure is one nasty-looking guy."

"Dad. He probably won't—"

"Ah," Drog said. "This must be the charming Mr. Lockwood, best known for the space he no longer occupies. What brings you to town, a sudden daddy-attack?"

"Drog!" I yelled and tried to stuff him back in my pocket. But Dad took hold of my wrist.

"Please, Dad."

"No. Let's hear everything this ugly puppet has to say."

"Everything?" said Drog. "Wheee! Don't get me started."

Dad tightened his grip. "I don't see its mouth moving, Parker."

"It's not, he . . ."

"It's snot!" Drog said and cackled.

Dad's eyes turned a harder blue.

"Please, Dad, let me . . ."

"Let's face it, Daddy-O." Drog said. "Parker and his mom, they were your practice family, no? And now you've got a new wife and a new kid, and you've got it *down*. So Parker's just kind of an embarrassing first try, am I right?"

Dad jerked back like he'd been punched. "No! Parker! How can you think that?!"

"Want me to answer that?" said Drog.

"Please, Dad. Let go!"

Instead he grabbed Drog with his other hand and tried to rip him off. Of course he couldn't. Dad glared at me, then looked away and loosened his grip.

"Listen, Mr. Lockbrain," Drog said. "You want my advi—" But by that time I had him back in my pocket.

Dad sat for a long time with his arms hanging at his sides, staring off across the ball field. I felt like I'd had my breath knocked out. I guess he did too.

"See what I mean, Dad?" I finally said. *See what I've been going through?*

He turned back to me and said in a husky voice, part angry, part . . . I didn't know what, "Parker, we've obviously got some big problems here, and it looks like they're going to be harder to work out than I thought. But one thing I've never seen from you until today is disrespect. I'm not used to that, and I'm not going to get used to it."

"But Dad, I didn't say anything. It was—"

"You know what would have happened to me if I had talked like that when I was a kid?"

I shook my head.

"My mother would have sent me to my room for a week."

I fought not to cry. "How about your dad?" I said. "What would your dad have done?"

"Well, he'd certainly have demanded an apology."

A tear got loose, and I wiped it off my face "I'm really sorry, Dad," I said. "Drog . . . shouldn't have talked to you that way."

Dad sighed and rested his hand on my knee. "Okay, Son," he said, "if that's the best you can do. Apology accepted. But can you promise me it won't happen again?"

I couldn't. How could I?

"Parker?"

"No."

"Get in the car," he said.

Neither of us spoke on the way home. This time the brown-spice smell of him practically suffocated me. Everything was so wrong, so unfixable. I rolled down the window for some cold air.

Dad pulled into the driveway but kept the engine running. "We both know this can't go on," he said, looking straight out the window. "Your mother asked me to be patient while you and the doctor try to figure out why you're doing this. I am trying, Parker."

He turned toward me then, but I couldn't look at him.

"I wanted to help you today. But you have to let me. And you have to try, too. If things don't get a lot better soon, I'm going to have to do something myself. This just can't go on."

I got out of the car and stood there as he backed out. He raised his hand in a small, sad wave. It was a minute before I could raise mine back, but by that time he'd turned out of the driveway, and I wasn't sure he saw me do it. I wanted him to see. He had to! I ran out to the street, with my hand high, high. The back end of his car, huge in front of me at first, got smaller and smaller down the street until it turned into a dot moving north on a map toward Moline.

chapter seventeen

I couldn't just go in the house. I had to do something or I'd explode. I paced back and forth in the backyard for awhile but the pressure just built up worse. I leaned up against the crabapple tree and yanked Drog out, ripping my pocket.

"Well, well. We really told old Daddy-O, didn't we?" he said.

"Shut your stupid, stupid mouth!" I said through gritted teeth. "Thanks to you, my dad might never talk to me again."

"Well, you're welcome. I—"

"Just shut UP!" I screamed and whacked his mouth against the tree, hard. Then I did it again. Let him squeeze my hand clear off, I didn't care.

"Hurt me, hurt yourself," Drog said in a shaky voice.

I made my puppet hand into as much of a fist as I could. *Blam!* I hit the tree straight on.

I didn't feel anything for a minute, and then . . . Drog was right. It hurt bad.

"My head is bl-bloody, but unbowed," Drog whispered.

He didn't squeeze my hand. Maybe he was still too stunned. A little blood did trickle down out of the puppet glove, but that had to be mine. I watched it run down my arm.

I wasn't finished. I ran into the house and charged up the stairs to my room. If Drog was my total enemy, I didn't owe him anything. Nothing. What he just did to me and my dad gave me every right to put an end to him. Even if he could talk. I snatched the scissors off my desk.

"Been there, done that, no?" Drog said.

"No! Because this time I'm really cutting you off."

I stuck one blade of the scissors into the puppet sleeve and squeezed the handle. Nothing. I squeezed again, and again, until my hand cramped. Why couldn't I cut? It was only cloth, but I might as well have been trying to cut rock. The scissors broke apart on the next squeeze, and I threw the two halves across the room.

"Hmmm," Drog said. "Looks like Drog has learned to focus his *ki* energy, no?"

I flopped back onto my bed and closed my eyes.

"Why fight it so hard, Boy?" Drog said. "We're a pretty good team when you think about it."

I silenced him with a pillow, because my hand was throbbing too much to put him back in my pocket.

What if my hand swells up inside him and gets infected? I thought. *What could anybody do about it?*

The next thing I knew, Mom was sitting on the edge of my bed. "It's after six," she said. "I got home an hour ago, but I let you sleep because you looked so wiped out. You okay?"

I shook my head and she felt my forehead. I guessed no infection had set in yet, because she didn't go for the thermometer. But I kept Drog under the pillow in case there were any bloodstains showing.

"Want to tell me what happened today?"

Tell her what Drog said about her and me? Tell her what Dad said? No way.

"Oh, Drog mouthed off at Dad and he thought it was me talking." True.

Mom put her hand over her eyes for a minute, then took them away and worked up a smile. "I don't feel much like fixing supper so late," she said. "Let's go for pizza."

"Thanks, Mom, but I'm not very hungry."

"Well, I am," she said. "Keep me company?"

I waited until she went for her coat, then wrapped Drog in the Ace bandage.

Once we got to Pizza Dan's, I did manage to put away three slices of pepperoni. Which was probably good because my hand was going to need food to heal.

We finished up, but then we just sat at the table like neither of us really wanted to leave and go back home. I looked at Mom. She looked at me.

"Tell me again why Dad left us," I said.

I didn't want to hear any divorce-for-kids version, and I guess she could tell. She wiped the table with the napkin. Twice.

"At first it was all about work. Your dad was supposed to be the chief engineer for building an overpass out on East Main that would keep the trains from stopping traffic all the time. It was a project he'd dreamed of since he was a teenager."

"But they never did that."

"No. The funding fell through and they abandoned the project. For a while he was pretty depressed and hard to live with. Then one day, without consulting me or even telling me, he applied for the job in Moline. And took it. A great opportunity, he said.

"That was March. I had three weeks to quit my job at the library, get the house ready for sale, pull you out of school, and move to Moline, where we didn't know anyone. I said no. We had to wait at least until the end of the school year."

"So he went without us."

"Yes."

"I remember him coming and going for a while."

"He came home on weekends, whenever he wasn't tied up at work. Then it got to be summer, and I kept putting off moving. Then fall. That winter, he came home less and less. He said I apparently loved my job and you and Ferrisburg more than I loved him."

One-point one-point one-point. "Did you?"

She looked at me in shock. "Well, I . . ." She didn't finish. She didn't have to.

"So it wasn't all Dad's fault," my voice said. The rest of me just felt . . . hollow.

Mom's eyes flickered. "It wasn't really anyone's fault, Parker. It certainly wasn't yours."

I wanted to believe that, but it was easy math. If Mom had loved Dad a little more or me a little less, then one plus one plus one would still equal three. Together. Any way you looked at it, I was a factor.

As soon as we got home, Mom punched the phone machine and Dad's voice said, "This message is for Parker."

She ducked out of the room.

"Parker?" the voice said. "We didn't have a very good afternoon did we? But what I'm really concerned about is those things you said. They're not true, believe me. I want you to know that." He was quiet a minute, then he said "Goodnight, Son."

Goodnight, not goodbye.

chapter eighteen

My Drog hand didn't swell up after all, but otherwise things sure didn't look like they were going to get better. So what did Dad mean when he said he'd have to do something? What would a guy like Dad do if he thought his son was making things up and being disrespectful and being allowed to get by with it? Why not send him off to Bradley, his favorite military school?

Bradley. I'd heard all the stories and driven by it sometimes in the car, but what was it really like? What did I know about it? Nothing.

Sunday morning was gray and gusty, but I wrapped Drog in the Ace bandage, got on my bike, and rode across town to check Bradley out, to see what I might be up against. I felt weird about pedaling up to the place, so I locked my bike to a tree a block away and walked, leaning into the wind.

The fence around Bradley looked like a row of iron spears stuck in the ground point-up. I peeked through the gate. The grass inside was all brown, but still cut short and neat. A box that looked like a tollbooth was empty. The word *sentry* popped into my head. That must be it.

Lights were on in a few big stone buildings, but there didn't seem to be anybody around. Then, out of nowhere, a car came down the drive. The gate opened by itself, and I jumped out of the way. All I could see was the driver's uniform before the gate closed behind him again with a click and he was gone.

I peered back through the bars. Just to the side of the driveway stood a big statue, the same grey-black as the fence. Shiny—like when you rub hard with a pencil. It was of a man in a real old-fashioned-looking uniform. I couldn't read the words on the base, and the wind had blown a piece of newspaper over the face and stuck it there, but I figured this must be a statue of some general named Bradley that the school was named after. I was just trying to figure out if there was any way I could get inside when a gust ripped the paper off the statue's face.

Except it wasn't a face. It wasn't even a human head. It was the head of a bird, an eagle.

I wanted to yell. I wanted to run, but I couldn't get my legs to move. I could only stare at that fierce man-bird. I couldn't stand being there alone with that thing, but the schoolyard and the street behind me were both empty.

Why hadn't I brought someone with me?

Drog! As fast as I could with my hand shaking, I unwound the Ace bandage.

"Wha—? Where are we?" Drog said, waking up.

I pointed his face toward the statue. Drog clenched.

"It's HIM," he screamed. "Run for your life!"

Suddenly my legs unfroze and I tore down the street, with the end of the bandage streaming behind my Drog hand, all the way back to my bike.

"What do you mean, 'it's him'?" I said, catching my breath. "Who?"

"Ben-Ra, you fool! The phantom-maker! He can suck people's brains out through their eye-sockets just by looking at them. Been doing it for thousands of years. Aiya! You didn't look directly at him did you?"

"I . . . I don't think so."

"Well, then maybe we're safe, but let's get going!"

I got on my bike and headed home. "Take it easy, Drog," I said. "That really scared me too, but it's a statue. Somebody made it. It couldn't have been there thousands of years."

"You don't understand, Boy. Ben-Ra takes many *forms*. Didn't you hear him? He said 'I smell a puppet and his boy!' It's Ben-Ra, I tell you!"

By the time he decided we were safe at home, Drog was wiped out by all the stress of the afternoon. He fell asleep, slept through supper, and snored all night.

It wasn't so easy for me. Of course Drog had to be talking crazy about the statue being a brain-sucker, but I was still shaking, thinking about that head.

I asked Mom if she knew anything about a creepy statue at Bradley Military, and she said she'd never paid any attention. I knew I couldn't have imagined that eagle. I looked up the B.M. website, but I couldn't find a picture of it. There was a map, though, and right about where the man-eagle should be were the words "Homage to Valor." That must be what the statue was called. I looked up the words and they meant something like honoring courage. Maybe it was a test you had to pass to be a Bradley cadet.

Maybe you had to be able to walk by that thing without flinching to enter the academy. I would fail that test for sure. Part of me swore I would never ever look at that terrible statue again if I could help it. But part of me was tempted to go back and make a drawing of it. From across the street.

That night in bed, sharp beak shapes kept poking into my hands and spoiling the patterns I was trying to make in my mind. Beaks and claws and lightning bolts. I tried to move them around, too, but they were like magnets that came together on their own, forming an iron mask too cold to touch.

chapter nineteen

"Well, well, looky who's here," Drog said.

Notebook Man was back on the playground on Monday, but this time he was going up to the sixth-graders one by one, bending over to ask them questions and jotting down their answers. The weird thing was, the kids he talked to didn't report to the rest of us, they just tried to pretend nothing happened.

Talk about energy coming out of people! The whole schoolyard felt like a wind-up toy cranked as far as it would go. Or maybe it was just me. I guessed I'd have to wait until it was my turn.

It never was my turn, because Wren went over to Mrs. Belcher and said something, and Mrs. Belcher stormed over to Notebook Man with her porcupine quills out.

"*Mister* Masterson!" she said.

He stopped writing, straightened up, and tried to smooth a few hairs over his forehead with the heel of his hand. Mrs. Belcher shooed away the kids around them and said some more stuff to him that no one else could hear, and when she was finished he snapped his notebook shut and left. She kept her hands on her hips until he was out of sight.

When the bell rang for the end of recess, I felt like it went off in my brain.

"Don't ask me, I'll tell you," Wren said when we got back in the room. "That man who's been writing—"

"Notebook Man?" I said.

Her eyes smiled for a second.

"Well, he wanted to know all about the puppet. And he asked a lot of other questions. About you."

"About me? Like what?"

"Like how long you've been acting this way and what we thought it was all about and whether you have any friends."

One-point one-point one-point. "What did you say?"

"I said I was your friend."

I closed my eyes.

"And I said I thought you were normal."

I opened my eyes again. "Do you?"

"I don't know."

"Well, thanks for saying that anyway."

"He said not to tell, but I don't like secrets like that."

"Thanks, Wren. Thanks for telling me."

Great. Nobody's talking to me, they're just talking about me. And they think I'm crazy.

I expected Wren to go to her seat then, but she hung around, turning her pocket stone over and over in one hand. "Parker, you know what my mom says?"

"What?"

"She says it's natural for boys and girls our age to go their own ways, even if they've been friends before. She thinks that's all that's happening."

Natural? Natural? How could anything be more unnatural than Drog? "That's not what's happening, Wren."

"I know. But I think I've got it figured out." She sounded half-sad, half-teasing.

"Uh oh," I said, trying to tease back. "Again?"

"Yep. You're not really Parker at all. They've taken him away, and you're an alien that replaced him."

I had to smile. "Well, I've got the green hand, anyway."

She started to smile back and then stopped. "Whoever you are, I want you to bring Parker back."

My eyes stung and I turned away. I said something dumb like "I'll see what I can do."

An alien. Well, that was one I hadn't thought of. Sure would explain why Drog would glom onto me. Takes one to know one. Or maybe it was the other way around—by attaching himself to my hand, Drog was slowly turning me into an alien like him. So how do you stop being an alien?

"Alien, eh?" Drog said. "Ever wonder if they eat Mars Bars on Mars, Boy?"

Dad. Notebook Man. Wren. I could hardly wait to get to aikido that day. The dojo was beginning to be the one place I could feel okay and relax.

"Don't go tonight. Trust me." Drog said as I reached for my *gi*. "Any fool could see what's going on at that dodo."

"Dojo. What do you mean? What's going on?"

"Think about it. You dress in white uniforms and bow to the master and speak only when spoken to—even Big Boy, the torch murderer. A room full of boys and girls sitting on their heels, bowing and being respectful and meditating about peace and harmony? It's unnatural."

"But—"

"And look what they teach you. You actually have to practice giving up. They plan to make you into zombies, I tell you. Probably some kind of cult!"

"Drog, that's silly."

"Silly, ha! Someone attacks you and you're supposed to do nothing?"

"Sometimes. At least until you figure out what's happening."

"So in your case I suppose that would mean doing nothing for a lifetime."

"Listen, Drog," I said, "I'm going to keep on going to aikido practice. If you don't like it, take a nap or something."

"My, my, aren't we getting testy? What would Pansy say?"

"It's Sensei, Drog! And you know what? Someday I'm going to figure out what makes you talk, and then I'm going to turn you OFF."

"Ha, ha. That's funny, Boy. Nothing *makes* me talk. I say what I please when I please. Which is a lot more than I can say for you."

Drog kept up his aikido-bashing on the way to practice.

"Don't you get it?" he said. "Aiki-dodo is like sword fighting on the stage. Looks great, but it's all rehearsed. You do this and I'll do that and it'll all come out here. Easy! Useless! In a real-life fight, you think the opponents cooperate and try not to hurt each other? No way! It's anything goes!"

Just then I thought I saw Wren going into the dojo ahead of me. It was her.

"Good grief," Drog said. "Too many girls. Girls would never be allowed at Shaolin."

Wren was already wearing her *gi*, so she'd planned this. She'd probably read a book about it. Aikido practice was supposed to be my break from thinking about problems, including my problems with her. But here she was.

What was she doing anyway, competing with me? Oh well, if she stuck it out, maybe she'd at least see how people treated each other in the dojo. How they treated me.

I half-waved to her.

"Good," Sensei said. "You know each other."

I couldn't get over her being there. "How come you signed up for aikido, Wren?"

She shrugged and looked at Sensei. "I guess if you can't beat 'em, join 'em."

Sensei grinned. "Exactly! Parker, please take Wren to the side mat and show her the beginning roll."

Wren frowned. "No," she said.

"No?"

Whoa, Wren.

"What I mean is, not with Drog."

"We can't always choose our opponents, Wren," Sensei said in a kind voice. "Please step onto the mat."

We took our positions. *Forget about everything but aikido,* I said to myself.

"I can't believe Sensei lets you practice with Drog on," Wren said.

I put my hand on my one-point for a moment, breathing out. Then I focused on rolling, rolling. When I finished, I bowed to Wren without thinking. I felt Sensei smile behind me.

Wren tried the roll. At first she ended up flat on her back, but she caught on pretty quick. I went a half step ahead and showed her how to push down on my wrist to make me roll. Then I did the same with her with my good hand, not hard.

After a while, Sensei called everybody over to talk about centering on our one-point. That was mostly for Wren, but he said the rest of us could never hear it too often.

Wren's mom offered me a ride after class, but I had my bike so I said no. Besides, I wanted to talk to Sensei alone. I walked around with him while he locked up.

Say something, I thought. But what? Tell him I got my dad all insulted and then beat up my puppet?

"Something awful happened Saturday," I blurted out. "My . . . somebody got mad at me for something I didn't do, and then everything got worse and worse. I sure could have used my one-point then, but I didn't think about it. Not even once."

He nodded. "That can happen."

"Sensei," I said, "do you ever let things really get to you and, you know, lose your center?"

He nodded again. "Often!"

"But—"

"The important thing is to find it again quickly when you need it."

He unrolled the mat again, stepped out of his shoes and commanded, "Kata Mochi!"

That was a technique we had just been working on during practice.

Without thinking, I kicked my shoes off too and got in position. I knew I was supposed to grab his shoulder, and then he would take my wrist, move in toward me, and turn

149

me to the side and down to the mat. But just then I remembered what Drog had said about it all being too easy. *What if I do something else?* I thought. *Something Sensei doesn't expect?*

I pretended to reach for his shoulder but I kicked high instead, aiming for his chest like I had seen street fighters do in the movies. Sensei's eyes widened, but he ducked before I could connect, then pushed on my shoulder and turned me until I ended up behind him on my knees.

I got up and we faced each other again. I thought he might be mad about what I had done, but he just stood there, ready.

Everything tormenting me came together in that moment. Not being able to get my hand out of Drog prison. Not being believed when I told the truth. Constantly getting on everyone's bad side even though I wasn't doing anything wrong.

Something inside me switched on and I exploded — punching, shoving, butting, swinging, tripping—and yelling and grunting with each thrust. No matter what I tried, though, or which way I turned, his body swirled around me like a river whose current was so strong I had to go where it took me, while his face seemed to stay still in the middle, growing calmer and calmer.

Finally I gave up, breathless, and stood up.

"When you prevent someone from hurting you, you do him a favor," Sensei said, quietly.

I nodded.

I put my hand on his shoulder and he turned me down to the mat in one motion. Then he helped me up and bowed to me. I bowed back.

"Don't worry, Parker," he said. "Things get easier with practice."

We rolled the mat back up, then he held the front door for me and set the bolt.

I was halfway home before I realized Sensei never asked me what it was that went wrong. All he ever talked about was practice. Well at least there was one person I couldn't hurt even if I tried. And Drog was wrong about aikido.

chapter twenty

In the middle of a math quiz I'd barely studied for, I watched Wren sharpen her pencil for the tenth time. She'd smell like pencil shavings by the end of the day. She gets all nervous about quizzes and can't think about anything else until they're over. Not me. My problem is making myself concentrate instead of doodling on the page.

"You're a null set yourself," Drog said. "You forgot to carry the three."

He was right. I erased my answer and changed it.

We went through the quiz like that. Drog making remarks, me changing my answers.

Mrs. Belcher looked up. "Please, Parker. No talking during a quiz."

Drog actually had the sense to whisper after that.

I turned in my paper with corrections on almost half the problems. And no doodles.

It was getting kind of cold to go out for recess, but Mrs. Belcher doesn't let us stay in unless it's at least twenty below. We need exercise every day, she says, and we sure get it in the winter, because if you stood still you'd have to be carried back inside in a frozen block. You don't exactly feel like playing games, though. You mostly just run around flapping your arms.

I saw somebody moving over behind the hedge where we're not supposed to go. I walked around the end and there was Big Boy, practicing his aikido moves. He motioned me over. Then he surprised me with a throw and I rolled as well as I could in my winter jacket. I threw him back.

A window creaked open. "You boys wouldn't be fighting on the school grounds would you, by any chance?"

It was Mr. Fairweather. I slipped Drog into my pocket.

"No, sir," Big Boy said. "This here's something else, not fighting."

"Hmmmm. I'm not even going to ask. Well, get on back to your room. Recess is over."

"I have some good news," Mrs. Belcher said later that afternoon. "Two people got perfect scores on the math quiz. Wren Rivera and . . . Parker Lockwood! Congratulations, Parker. No careless errors. No errors, period!"

Wren turned around and looked at me like I'd shot her with a paint gun.

She stopped me going out the door after school.

"How did you get so good in math all of a sudden?"

"Want to know the truth?"

"Of course. Did you cheat?"

Okay, here goes the truth. "Yeah, in a way. It's Drog. Drog corrected my mistakes for me."

"Oh right. Just when I think . . . Am I supposed to pretend I believe that? You're impossible."

That made me mad. "Well how about you, Miss Perfect? You just can't stand it if somebody does as well as you. It's not enough for you to be good, you have to be the only one!"

Me and my big mouth.

"That's telling her," Drog said, but I just stood there watching Wren walk away. Again.

I didn't feel right accepting that perfect score, so I hung around until all everyone had left and went back into the room.

"Um, Mrs. Belcher?"

She looked up and beamed at me. "Yes, Parker?"

"I . . . didn't exactly do that well on the quiz by myself. I . . . had some help."

"Oh?" Her smile shrank to a zero.

"That was Drog talking during the quiz, telling me my mistakes."

Mrs. Belcher smiled even bigger than before. I could tell she was trying not to laugh.

"Well, if it's only Drog," she said. "Did he also tell you the answers?"

"No, just where I went wrong. Then I fixed it."

Now she did laugh a little. "Parker, I appreciate your telling me this," she said. "But I don't think there's a problem here, do you? Drog is a part of you after all, so if he knows how to do a problem, it means you do."

"But—"

"You tell Drog, whatever he's doing, to keep it up. And I'll look for improvement in your homework."

So I wasn't in trouble. But Mrs. Belcher's awful words filled my brain: *Drog is a part of you, after all . . .*

———

Outside, Gordy and some of the guys were bouncing a ball off the side of the building and talking. I waved, but they didn't see me, and then I heard my name. I backed up close to the wall around the corner from them and listened.

Ka-whonk!

"So how long do you think he's going to keep this up?"

"As long as he wants, I guess."

As long as I want? Did they think I liked being a puppet's puppet?

"Can you believe how nice Mrs. Belcher is being about it? Most kids would be suspended by now."

"Hey, I know," Gordy said. "Maybe it's some kind of school experiment or something. Like he's supposed to do this. To see how everybody will react. And Mrs. Belcher and Mr. Fairweather and the principal are all in on it."

Well, at least Gordy thinks I might not be crazy.

Ka-thonk!

"I've seen him talking to Big Boy. Think Big Boy's part of it?"

"Could be. Nobody talks to Big Boy."

Right. Maybe somebody should try it sometime.

"And what about that man who came around asking questions? I didn't tell him anything."

Blam.

"Me neither. Didn't like him."

Thanks, guys.

"I bet that magazine job was just a cover. He's probably FBI. Or CIA."

"Yeah. What if the puppet's wired? It doesn't just talk, it eavesdrops for some foreign government or something, and—"

"Yeah, and the guy on the playground was a counterspy trying to find out what they know."

Wow, if Mom thinks I let my imagination run away with me, she should listen to this!

"So, you think Parker's a spy, too?"

What?

"Nah. They're probably just making him cooperate. Where's his dad, anyway? Maybe they've got him."

"Or maybe his dad's part of it—"

I had to stop this. I came around the corner like I hadn't heard anything and said "Hi. Wanna play dodge ball?"

I couldn't believe how fast they all said "Hi, Parker" and "Sure."

It was funny but it wasn't. Because they had me thinking again about Notebook Man. Drog had called him a spy from the beginning, Could he actually be right in a way? Why *did* Notebook Man zero in on Drog and me? What did he know that I didn't know, and what was he trying to find out? Could he have gotten me into some big trouble? Good thing Mrs. Belcher ran him off.

Thanksgiving came, and it was great to have nothing but turkey and aikido to think about. At practice we weren't just rolling anymore, we were learning to fall from a standing position, forward and backward.

Sensei paired Big Boy and Wren and me with other students, not each other. But I kept an eye on Wren whenever I stopped to rest. She did okay with the throws, but when it was her turn to fall, especially backwards, she got all messed up and mad at herself. She just couldn't let herself fall. Except when Sensei was her partner.

Big Boy could fall for anybody, even though he had the farthest to drop. I was somewhere in between but getting better. The more you relax, the easier it is. Why couldn't Wren see that? I wondered.

That Saturday, Big Boy called me up. He wanted me to meet him at the mall and see a Jackie Chan movie. He'd heard Jackie Chan did all his own martial-arts stunts.

It had been a while since I'd been in a movie theater with anybody besides Wren or Mom. We got a big bag of popcorn and took seats in the back. Big Boy held the bag, and I helped myself with my good hand.

The kung fu was fantastic. It couldn't happen the way it showed in the movie, of course, but it was great to watch Jackie go after the bad guys. One head-cracking scene that left three evil ninjas groaning on the ground reminded me of Drog and me.

"You think Sensei would like this movie?" I said to Big Boy.

He laughed. "No way, man!"

"You gonna tell him we saw it?"

"Nah."

We broke up laughing.

That day at aikido we had to concentrate extra hard on our one-points and not look at each other so we wouldn't remember the movie and laugh out loud in the middle of practice.

Monday after Thanksgiving we started basketball in P.E. Our gym has special baskets built for about fourth-graders. By the time you're a sixth-grader you can hit them easy. And Big Boy could practically do a standing slam dunk.

I could steady the ball with my Drog hand and dribble with my right. But I could hardly catch, except when Big Boy threw the ball, and I couldn't pass or shoot for anything. I used to be chosen third or fourth for a team, but nobody wanted me anymore. I could see why. I gave up and went back to the climbing wall. Couldn't do much there either, except hang by one arm and watch everybody else play.

Mrs. Belcher let me be in the first group to go on the computers when we got back to the room. We were supposed to be coming up with ideas for our science projects so we'd be ready to start after Christmas, but I decided to do a search on one-armed people.

I found a tournament for one-armed golfers, and a thirteen-year-old champion surfer who went back to competition a couple of months after a shark bit off her arm. I found famous pianists who lost a hand or arm in wartime but still played one-handed pieces composers wrote especially for them. I even found a story about a black woman and a white woman who each loved to play the piano, but one had a stroke on her left side and the other had a stroke on the right. You guessed it, they heard about each other and got together to play. They even performed, calling themselves "Ebony and Ivory." No kidding.

I guess those stories should have inspired me. More like the opposite. They made me think about how everybody, including me, was getting used to the idea that I had only one hand.

The longer Drog stayed on, the more I felt like I might not ever have fun again, like I'd already made everything I was ever going to make and it wasn't enough.

chapter twenty-one

As I was leaving school, I heard shouting over in the corner of the playground. Some older boys were yelling at a bunch of our kids. A couple of them looked familiar—guys from Bradley Military who'd come around before. The biggest one had Charlie Sloat by the front of his jacket and was lifting him off the ground. The security guard was nowhere around, and I was the only sixth-grader. I headed over.

"What's happening?" I asked one of the kids standing there watching.

"That's Wade Hunt. Some fifth-graders went over to his house over Thanksgiving and TPed the bushes."

"Really?"

"Yeah. And they left a big sign in the middle that said B.M. Happens."

I laughed. "Good for them. That's funny."

"Well, Wade isn't laughing."

Just then Wade Hunt turned Charlie upside down and started shaking him like a ketchup bottle. "You're nothing but a little turd yourself," he said. "I'd flush you down the toilet, but you'd probably clog it up. Guess I'll just have to dispose of you in the trash can."

"No!" yelled Drog.

Charlie opened his mouth to yell, but nothing was coming out.

"Cut that out," I called to Wade. "How do you even know it was him?"

He turned. "I know. Just look at him. So guilty."

"So scared. Can't you tell the difference?"

"Go for him!" hissed Drog.

"Put Charlie down," I said to Wade.

"Yeah," Charlie's friends said, lining up behind me.

I pictured my feet planted in the ground with mile-long roots.

Wade turned to faced me. "Oh, you want to fight me, Mop Head? No problem."

I checked out his hands and his chest. He was pretty big.

"You can beat him, Boy," Drog said. "He doesn't know your tricks. Go on, he deserves it."

I started toward Wade with my hands up.

He dropped Charlie like a sack and stepped forward. "Hey, what's that thing on your hand?" he said.

"It's a puppet. What did you think?"

"Well take it off. I'm not fighting with a puppet."

"No, you're fighting with me!"

I shoved him in the chest, but he grabbed both my wrists quicker than I thought he could. Up close, he was even bigger.

Doesn't matter, I can do this. It's just like practice.

It wasn't. I spread my elbows and raised my hands to duck to the side. That was supposed to make him turn too, or risk getting his wrist broken. But he just stood there and grinned. I hated that look.

I went slack, then lunged forward with my right arm and punched him in the eye, catching him by surprise, so I could finally turn him. I yanked my hands free and pushed down on his elbow. He dropped to the ground in a second, and I held his arm behind his back.

He didn't get up. At first I thought maybe I had really hurt him instead of just wanting to. But then I realized he didn't want to show his face because he was crying. Too bad. I wanted to twist his arm until it cracked.

I looked up. The other B.M. guys were standing there with their mouths hanging open.

"Who's next?" Drog said. "Leave no survivors!"

"Shut up, Drog."

Someone took hold of my arm.

"What're you doing, man?" It was Big Boy.

I let go of Wade, but he stayed facedown.

The B.M. guys pulled him to his feet and dragged him off. He kept both his eyes covered, even though I'd only hit one.

I stood up.

Then our kids got brave, calling after the guys: "B.M. got flushed! B.M. got flushed!"

I heard them from far away though, like it was just Big Boy and me on the playground. Him looking at me. Me looking back.

"What're you doing?" he said again, real low, and let go of me.

I turned away a minute and said, "You okay, Charlie?"

Charlie brushed the dirt off his pants. "Yeah, I guess. Thanks, Parker. Thanks a lot."

When I turned back, Big Boy had already walked away.

One of the fifth-grade girls said, "You're a hero, Parker."

A hero? Inside, I was dizzy and shaking. Scared, but not of Wade Hunt. Scared of how much I had really wanted to hurt him. Sure, he was a jerk, but that wasn't why. I didn't know why.

"Well, well," crooned Drog on the way home. "So all that aikido practice was good for something after all."

"You think so? I didn't have to get into that fight."

"Nonsense! It was the honorable thing to do. He was about to put that boy in the trash can!"

"It wasn't self-defense. It wasn't a matter of life and death."

"Speak for yourself."

"Fighting is stupid, Drog. It just leads to more fights."

"That's the law of the jungle gym, Boy. You're king of the mountain. Get used to it."

"You don't understand."

"No, *you* don't understand. The kiddies at this school will follow you around like ducks now. If you've got the blame you might as well have the game."

I decided maybe I'd skip aikido that night.

"So, Parker, you becoming a frequent flyer?" Mr. Fairweather said first thing the next morning.

"What do you mean?"

"I mean this is the second time you've been sent to see me in a month. They say you've gone from puppet handling to fistfights. Tell me all about it."

I told him the main facts.

"Oh sure, I know that kid. Used to go here, in fact. Got a chip on his shoulder the size of the Sears Tower."

He leaned over the desk and lowered his voice.

"I'm going to have to send you to the cafeteria for a little K.P. duty this morning, Parker. And I've called your mom. Zero tolerance for fighting at school and all that. But just between you and me, I'm sure the guy had it coming."

I headed out the door with my pass, but he called after me. "Still got that thing on? Doesn't it, you know, get in the way of the old one-two punch?"

I held up my free hand. "It only took one," I said, and he leaned back in his chair, laughing.

Drog was right. The little kids did hang on me on the playground that afternoon. It was pretty embarrassing. One boy even had a puppet on his hand.

Big Boy came right up to me at the dojo that day.

"Come to aikido, you told me. You can fight but not get mad, you said. You stay cool. So what about you, man?" Big Boy said.

I looked down. "I guess . . . I kind of lost it. I wanted to hurt him."

"How'd you get into that fight anyway?" he said. "I didn't see it start."

"I was the one who started it. I shoved him."

"What for?"

"He was bullying Charlie. He . . . I didn't hurt him much."

I looked up. There was Sensei, standing behind Big Boy. He'd heard everything. I bowed to him, and when I lifted my head he looked right between my eyes.

Sensei began practice by talking about doing things with intention.

"Whether something you do is weak or strong depends on your intention, because your energy goes where your intention is. If you do nothing, that could just be laziness or weakness or not being able to make up your mind. But if doing nothing is your intention, it can mean you're strong. In whatever you do, keep your intention and don't let your mind get scattered."

There were nine of us. Whenever there was an uneven number, Sensei always paired himself with somebody for practice, and everyone hoped it would be them. He paired the other eight, Big Boy with Wren, then he said, without looking at me, "And anyone else who feels like practicing can go to the side mat and review the beginning roll."

The beginning roll!

"That's an insult, boy!" Drog hissed. "What are you going to do about it?"

"I'm going to go over to the side mat and practice the beginning roll."

"After all you've learned?"

"Sensei doesn't think I've learned much."

"Ha! He's just trying to control you!"

Oh, right. Look who's talking.

The truth was, I *wanted* to practice that roll. It was something to do to keep from remembering the way Sensei looked right through me. My intention was to fall and roll all night and get into the rhythm of it so I wouldn't have to think.

I was still falling and rolling when everybody else had finished. Sensei didn't call me over to the mat for closing thoughts or even seem to notice that I kept going.

Everyone bowed and said good night to Sensei. But me, I was going to roll all night if nobody stopped me. Wren and Big Boy came by the side mat and watched for a minute, but they left without saying anything. And all I said to myself was *fall, roll, up, down, roll, up.*

Suddenly Sensei was rolling beside me, and when we came up together, he took hold of my shoulders and held me still.

I couldn't look at him.

"You attacked someone," he said.

I nodded.

"You defeated your opponent instead of turning him. You fought to win."

I nodded.

"You hurt him. You made an enemy."

Each thing he said felt like a cut. I nodded again and studied my big toe.

"That is not aikido."

"I'm sorry, Sensei."

"Yes. You showed that tonight. But now you must restore harmony."

I looked up. "How?"

"This person you attacked, this new enemy of yours. Take the one-down position with him."

"The one-down position?"

"Apologize to him. With your whole heart. Do not attempt to explain or excuse your behavior."

Apologize to Wade Hunt? I swallowed.

"If he criticizes you, agree with him. Accept humbly whatever he says and thank him. Remember he is your superior, because you have done him wrong."

"But he—"

"No matter what he did, he did not deserve to be forced to fight. That was your doing."

I made myself look up at him. "Thank you, Sensei, I'll . . . Thank you." I bowed to him.

His energy got softer and I thought everything was okay. Then he said, "Do not speak to me again until you have done this."

PART III

The Trouble With Practice

chapter twenty-two

Dad called that night.

"Your mother tells me you've been getting into fights."

"One fight. With a guy from B.M."

"From Bradley Military? Really? Why'd he pick on you?"

"Um, I started it, Dad."

"You did? You get hurt?"

"No."

"You picked a fight with a boy from Bradley Military and beat him?"

"I didn't beat him, exactly. I just hit him."

"Well, what do you know? I didn't realize you had it in you."

I shuddered. "Me neither."

"Well, what do you know?"

So Dad was suddenly kind of proud of me. For doing something that wasn't like me at all, something that Sensei didn't approve of. I couldn't win.

"Drog," I said as I was turning out the light, "Aikido is supposed to be about peace and harmony. Why can't I learn that?"

Whoa. Did I just ask a mean puppet for advice? Maybe I *was* crazy.

"You've been hanging around the dodo too much, Boy," he said. "You don't seem to realize we won that fight. You should be saying won point, won point!"

"Why didn't I find some other way?"

"Look, when the tough guy comes spoiling for a fight, he isn't going to leave until he gets it. You gave it to him. You beat him with one hand behind your back, shall we say, ha-ha! And now *you're* the tough guy. Simple."

"I don't want to be the tough guy."

"Listen to Drog for once. You want peace? Be so powerful nobody will dare attack you. Do you think the emir spent all his time fighting? No. A few heads lopped off from time to time and everyone got the message. Then he was free to spend time in his pleasure gardens."

I was so sick of hearing about that almighty emir I wanted to plunge him headfirst into a vat of his own gold-dust ice cream.

Still, I was starting to get used to talking with Drog. Even sitting still for his lectures, which was pretty weird. But who else besides me knew that he could talk on his own? That I wasn't crazy? Only somebody who believed that could have anything real to say to me about my problems. Of course he was also my biggest problem. That *could* make me crazy.

Wren caught up with me at the school crossing the next morning.

"I feel bad for you that Sensei's mad at you," she said. "I'd hate it if that happened to me."

I shrugged. "Yeah, well, maybe he's right."

"I don't understand why boys have to fight all the time. I always thought you were different. But ever since you put on that awful pup—"

"You're right, Wren," I interrupted. "It's no fun being on Sensei's bad side."

I didn't want to hear her say again what I knew she was thinking: why don't you just take the darn thing off?

At least there was Big Boy. He came over to my desk before the bell rang.

"I didn't tell you last night at practice because you were . . . kind of busy."

"Tell me what?"

"Remember that tall guy with the notebook? When you left school yesterday, he was there and he followed you. And I saw him again outside the dojo. Watch your back, man."

Notebook Man. Again? He hadn't been around school since Mrs. Belcher told him off that day. So why was he still hanging around? And why was he so darned interested in me?

I didn't go to aikido. With Wren giving me sad looks and Sensei giving me no looks, it just wasn't worth it. And if Notebook Man really was following me, he'd just have to take a night off.

Mom had a library meeting and left supper for me on the counter. So what did I end up doing? Watching TV and starting a few homework problems and wishing I was at aikido. Pathetic.

"No practice today?" Mom said when she got home.

"Didn't feel like it."

"Oh, did something happen?"

"Yes. No. Don't want to talk about it."

"I see. Want to watch a movie?"

"On a school night? You okay, Mom?"

"Uh-huh. Got much homework?"

"Just math. Drog can help me later. What movie?"

"You won't believe it. *Attack of the Killer Tomatoes!* Somebody donated it to the library today. I'll fix us some popcorn." Mom and I saw that movie once and laughed ourselves silly it was so bad.

Forget the microwave. Mom makes real popcorn on the stove in an old pan with the lid rattling. Then she melts butter to pour on it. Nothing tastes better than popcorn like that. Especially on a school night.

After one look at the opening scene, where a tomato comes muttering up out of the garbage disposal and corners the terrified housewife, Drog ordered me to put him in my pocket for the night.

But Mom and I chomped our popcorn and howled at the man-eating vegetables rolling off the counter and across the floor. And we cracked up crooning the words from the theme song: "I know I'm gonna miss her. A tomato ate my sister. . . ."

I felt so loose from all that laughing that I finished my math problems without much help from Drog. But when I turned out the light and got into bed, I ended up thinking about sisters. *I have a baby sister now, and I hardly ever see her. She's a half-sister to me. A whole daughter to Dad. And not a daughter or anything to Mom. How could that happen? I mean, I know, but how?*

I jumped out of bed, turned on the light, and opened my desk drawer.

"Wha . . . Wha . . ." Drog said.

"Something boring, Drog. Go back to sleep."

When he started to snore again, I felt around in the drawer until I found the envelope with the picture Dad had sent. A picture of Shanna. I slipped it out.

I don't know why people say a baby looks just like Aunt so-and-so, because to me babies don't look like anybody but themselves. Shanna looked cute and smart and silly, like somebody I might like to know, but not particularly like anybody I knew already.

Dad's hand propped her up for the picture. I kept looking at that hand, because I could tell, just from the way his thumb wrapped around her waist and his fingers pressed a little into her belly, how much he loved her. *He holds her that way every day. Was it ever like that with me?*

I put the picture away and tiptoed to the landing. Mom was on the couch, dozing into her book, so I went into her room and pulled open the bottom drawer where she kept the old family album. Lots of pictures of Mom and me in there, because Dad was the photographer. I flipped the pages until I found the one of Dad and me.

I couldn't tell anymore if I remembered that day or not, but I remembered the picture. Me on a sled, grinning out of my parka hood, and Dad riding behind me, grinning too, our cheeks red from the cold and our knees splotched with snow. Dad looked happy. Like there was nothing he'd rather be doing, nothing else on his mind. One of his hands spread across my chest, holding on. I could feel the warmth of it through my parka.

So he held me that way too, once.

What happened after that? Maybe kids are easier to like when they're little because they just are. Then they get too old to be cute, and their fathers start to worry about them and feel like they have to set an example and get them to do things right and it's not much fun anymore. But maybe if I'd been better at math . . .

I eased the picture out of the album and took it back to my room.

chapter twenty-three

Big Boy came over to my desk the next morning. "You weren't at practice yesterday."

"Did Sensei say anything?"

"No, but . . . he gave me and Wren progress certificates."

"What!"

"Yeah. You should have had yours before us. And you would've, if—"

"I hate this!" I said, slamming my desk with my fist. "I mean, good for you Big Boy, but—"

"Yeah. You and Sensei used to like each other. Maybe you should come back to class anyway."

"He'll just act like I'm not there."

"Well, do what you gotta do."

"What I have to do is apologize to Wade Hunt, no excuses. That's what Sensei says."

"That's rough, man."

I waited to eat lunch with Big Boy, but he said he was working with Mrs. Belcher again.

"You having trouble? Maybe I can help you."

"Nah, Mrs. B.'s working with me because I'm doing so good now! She says if I go to summer school, maybe I can get double promoted into eighth next year. Then I'll only be a year behind."

"That's great, Big Boy!" I said. Right then, I wished I had something else to call him.

Wren passed me a note during social studies:

Parker:
Tell your friend Drog it's not a boat, it's a poem.

Wren

I glanced up to see her holding up a faded red book and pointing to the cover. I turned away and pretended I wasn't interested.

As soon as Wren left school, I asked Mrs. Belcher if she knew anything about a famous ruby yacht.

"Oh, do you mean *The Rubaiyat of Omar Khayyam?*" she said.

"That's the one!" I said. "What . . . what is it?"

"It's a poem, Parker."

Oh no. "A poem?"

"Yes. A very long, very old Persian poem."

She wrote the title on the blackboard for me. "What a coincidence," she said, "Wren checked the book out from our library just today. I'm sure she would share it with you if you're interested."

Oh, I'm sure she would.

I thanked Mrs. Belcher and left.

"The Ruby Yacht is a poem, Drog," I said. "How come you told me it was a boat?"

He took his time. "Why of course it's a poem, Boy," he said in a too-high voice. "A poem . . . about the boat. Not at all surprising, do you think, that such a fabulous object should inspire poetry?"

"But it's spelled R-u-b-a-i-y-a-t. All one word."

"Hmmph! The reason should be obvious, even to you. That's simply how you write 'ruby yacht' in the Persian language."

Could that be right? I didn't know what to think. Use your head, Parker, Dad would say.

I did go back to the dojo that night. I wasn't too surprised when Sensei treated me like the Invisible Boy, but then I started to feel invisible. Over on the side mat, I tried some falls I had seen the older students do, where they fly through the air and slap the mat coming down. I wanted to feel that. To have it sting a bit so at least I would know I was there. Wren and Big Boy turned around a couple of times when I landed hard, but Sensei didn't.

I left after half an hour. He didn't pay any attention to that either.

I was going to have to do the one-down thing with Wade or quit aikido. I couldn't think which was worse, and my one-point mole wasn't sending me any clues.

"Wake up, Boy," Drog said when we got outside. "That Sensei is jerking your strings. All you have to do is give up all your self-respect and grovel in front of your enemy, right? Then you can come back to the doodoo and be his little pet again."

I yanked at a piece of paper that was stuck in my bike spokes.

"I don't need your opinion, Drog."

"Ha! That's what you think."

"Hey Drog! Look at this!"

The paper I had pulled out was an ad.

"GIRLS! GIRLS! GIRLS!" it said. "COME TO THE TITANIUM CLUB! LIVE EXOTIC DANCING NIGHTLY! (GENTLEMEN ONLY PLEASE)!"

It had a blurry picture of a woman leaning over a table. She didn't have a whole lot of clothes on.

I showed the paper to Drog.

"Aha! This is in Ferrisburg?"

"Uh-huh, out on Locust Boulevard."

"Wheee! Fun point, fun point! Well, what are we waiting for?"

"You mean *go* there? Now? But—"

"Don't tell me you're afraid?"

"No, but I'm supposed to —"

"Not as elegant as I would have expected," Drog said.

The Titanium Club was a low building, painted dark blue, with no windows. Light poured out from the doorway, though, and a man stood there, smoking a cigarette. He didn't see us.

I leaned my bike against a lamppost and stuck Drog in my pocket for the moment. Then I went up to the entrance.

The man barred the door with his arm.

"Where you going, kid?"

"We . . . I came to see the dancers."

"Nice try. They're not even on for three more hours. But you now, you need to come back in about ten years."

"Ten years?"

"Yep. This is strictly an adults-only establishment. Whooooeee! If I let a little greenhorn like you in here, they'd bust my— I'd be shut down before midnight. You better run along."

I walked back over to my bike.

He called after me, "Do your folks know where—what? You came here on a bicycle? Wait a minute. We'd better make sure you get home."

He pulled a phone from his belt and punched some numbers. In less than a minute, a policeman drove up on his motorcycle.

Uh-oh. It wasn't just any policeman, either. It would be Officer Dahl.

"This young man here came to the wrong place, Officer," the Titanium man said. "Probably didn't realize he was trespassing. Think maybe he needs an escort?"

Officer Dahl took a good look at me. "Say," he said, "aren't you Brian Lockwood's boy? Used to come downtown with your dad sometimes when he was working on the Simmons Street bridge project?"

I nodded. It must be the hair.

"Well, I'll be darned. What're you doing here, of all places? And on a school night?"

B.M. here I come.

I didn't answer.

"Get on your bike, son. You and I are going to ride along together to your place. Still live in that big old house on Prairie?"

I nodded again.

His blue motorcycle light flashed around and around. He was waiting. I had to take my Drog hand out if I was going to steer my bike.

"What's that you've got on your hand?" Officer Dahl said.

I held Drog up.

"Never mind. I don't think I want to know."

We headed down the street, me pedaling as fast as I could, and him cruising so slow he had to put his foot down every once in a while to keep from falling over. I prayed nobody I knew would see me.

When we got to my house, blue light still flashing, Mom rushed out onto the porch.

"What's wrong? What's happened?"

Officer Dahl put down his kickstand and walked toward her to shake hands.

"Evening, Mrs. Lockwood. Don't worry. Nobody hurt, nobody in trouble," he said. "Got a call from the doorman at the Titanium Club saying your son was there. Thought I'd better see him home safe."

"The Titanium Club! What on earth—"

"You're on your own, son," Officer Dahl said. He got back on his motorcycle, revved it, and rode off.

Mom herded me inside.

"The Titanium Club! You were supposed to be at aikido!"

"I left early. Mom, you won't tell Dad about this, will you? Please?"

"Tell him what? That his son played hooky from aikido and had to have a police escort home from the Titanium Club? Not if I can help it! But I've got a couple of things to say to you, mister."

I could imagine.

She shuddered, reached for a sweater from the hook, and put in on, crossing her arms. "First of all, for a guy who's promised me he'd do his best to stay out of trouble, I wouldn't say you've been using very good judgment, would you? The Titanium Club? It's not just the awful place, it's—"

"Mom, it was Drog. He wanted—"

"No! You will not use that puppet as an excuse. It's you I'm talking to here. The fact is that without telling anyone where you were going, you went alone to a part of town where there aren't exactly a lot of people watching out for kids. You tried to get into a nightclub that's barely legal for adults. And you were riding your bike after dark in a strange neighborhood, with a pretty dim headlight, I notice. I'd say you were lucky Officer Dahl came along!"

"I'm sorry, Mom."

"If you're really sorry, nothing even close to this will happen again." She tried to button up her sweater. Her voice sounded sure, but her hand shook. "I'm hanging your bike up in the garage for the winter."

Good. She's thought of something to do. Take it easy, Mom.

"You can walk to aikido from now on. And anytime you're not at home, at school, or at aikido, you need to get to a phone and let me know where you are. Agreed?"

I nodded.

"What is all this about exotic dancers anyway?" she said. "First the Internet, then those videos in your room, now this?"

"It's not me, Mom, it's—oh, never mind."

I figured things couldn't get much worse, so I told her. "Someone's been following me."

She sank down on the couch.

"Oh, Parker," she said in a tired voice, "why would anyone follow you?"

"I don't know, but I know who it is. It's a man who came to our school and wrote things down in a notebook. Notebook Man."

"Parker, please don't do this."

"Do what? I thought you'd want to know if someone was following me."

"Of course I would, but . . . aren't you letting your imagination run away with you?"

I yanked off my jacket and threw it on the couch. "You don't have to believe me! Big Boy saw him. Ask Big Boy!"

I stomped up to my room and slammed the door. A second later, Wren's geode crashed to the floor. I groaned and picked it up. It was still in one piece, just a chip out of the edge and a couple of crystals cracked, but I put it in my sweatshirt drawer to be safe.

"What kind of country is this, that nobody is allowed to watch dancing girls until they're twenty-one?" Drog said.

"Shut up, Drog."

chapter twenty-four

On her way out to the library the next morning, Mom stopped and squinted at me like I was a page of blurry print she needed to read.

"I'm glad your appointment with Dr. Mann is Monday, Parker."

I called after her as she went out the door. "Mom, could you bring me a book back? *The Rubaiyat of Omar Khayyam?*"

Her eyebrows scrunched into a what-next look. "I guess so," she said. "We must have a copy. Is it for school or something?"

"Sort of."

"Not for school, for fools!" Drog said.

Mom shook her head and left.

"Gee thanks, Drog," I said. "That helps."

Saturday again. No Wren. No aikido. No bike. And Dr. Mann to look forward to. Wheee.

I went back to bed and lay there as long as I could stand it. Then I got up and went downstairs. Mom had left me a list of one-handed chores. And a ten-dollar bill to pick up some masking tape and staples at the hardware store.

I bit the top off of a banana and peeled the sides down with my teeth so I could eat it, then I started unloading the dishwasher, one dish at a time.

But my big job for the weekend was to decide.

What would be so bad about quitting aikido? I really liked doing it, but maybe Drog was right about all the harmony and blending stuff. Aikido sure hadn't helped *me* lead a life of harmony. I'd never had so many people mad at me, and before aikido I'd never gotten into a real fight.

And how about awareness? All I seemed to be more aware of was the anger and worry and disappointment around me. And people following me.

Still, the dojo was the one place I could pretty much be myself, Drog and all. I wanted to be there with Wren and Big Boy. I just didn't want to go if Sensei disapproved of me.

I dragged the garbage can out to the street.

Why not just do what Sensei said? Shut my eyes and do it, like I was swallowing a maggot on a dare. Who cared what Wade Hunt thought, anyway? I might never see him again.

But Sensei said "with your whole heart." I was supposed to mean it, that was part of the deal.

Apologize to that jerk and treat him like he's right? How could I humiliate myself like that? I went into the mudroom and stomped on about a hundred soda cans to flatten them, then threw them one at a time into the recycling bin. Could Sensei himself do what he was telling me to? Well, Sensei wouldn't have gotten into a fight in the first place.

I took a break and heated some chocolate milk in a pan. Then I poured it into a mug, spilling some, and plopped a marshmallow into it. It was almost cocoa. I broke off a chunk of cheese and stuck it between two pieces of bread. It was almost lunch.

Something kept nagging me. Something about the fight. Aikido is self-defense, Sensei told us from the beginning. Fighting should be the last choice. Maybe there was no way I could have cooled things down and gotten Wade to leave Charlie alone, like Drog said.

But the truth was, I didn't even try. I really wanted to fight him. I was right to try to protect Charlie, and if Wade attacked me for that, I had the right to defend myself. But I was wrong to hit first.

I was definitely going to have to apologize. I gagged just thinking about it.

I grabbed my jacket and the ten dollars and headed for Carlson's Hardware. Mom could have picked up this stuff on her way home, but she probably wanted to make sure I got out of the house. Or maybe she thought a trip to the hardware store would get me going working on something.

I opened the front door at Carlson's and ran right into Wren's dad's chest. We both stepped back, and my face went hot. He shifted the package he was carrying to his other hand and searched me with his velvet eyes.

"Well, hello, Parker," he said. "Haven't seen you in a while. Been busy?"

I pulled Drog out long enough to show but shoved him back in my pocket before he could say anything.

"Yeah, kind of," I said.

Mr. Rivera nodded. So he knew. Wren told him. Of course.

We looked at each other some more.

"I've just finished putting the roof on Wren's house," he said. "You should see it. And I'm starting on a TV cabinet and some shelves for the Sloats. Come by sometime."

It felt like a question.

He waved and left the store.

I went home and dropped the bag of tape and staples on the kitchen table, then debated whether to watch a movie or play a video game, anything to keep from imagining facing Wade Hunt with "sorry" drooling out of my mouth. If only . . .

Oh just do it, Parker. Go! I zipped my jacket back up, scribbled a note to Mom and cut through the backyards to Wren's.

Almost lost my nerve, though, when I saw her bike leaning up against the side of the garage shop. I could hear the high-to-low whine of the power saw inside and the *plunk* of a sawn-off piece falling to the concrete. *Keep your intention, Parker.*

I stepped into the wedge of light coming from the doorway. Wren was leaning over the miniature house with a white plastic bottle and a brush in her hands. She looked up first, and the thought I saw flick across her face for a second almost made me turn around and leave. She wanted her dad to herself.

Wait, what if she'd always felt that way, and just shared him with me anyway because I was her friend? What about now?

Wren tried to smile. I lifted my chin to say, "Okay if I come in?"

She shrugged. "Papa, look who's here."

Mr. Rivera looked up then and broke into a grin. But he had heard something in Wren's voice, so he said, "Great! We could use some help. Right, *Corazon*?"

Wren just stood there with the bottle, so I walked over. At the base of the miniature house was a bucket of small pieces of wood. They had made grooves in each piece to look like shingles, and Wren was gluing them one by one onto the roof.

Without saying anything, she handed me the brush and showed me how much glue to brush on the end of a shingle and how to tuck it up under the last one. I couldn't get them in tight enough one-handed though, so she nudged me aside and redid them herself. I ended up just putting the glue on and handing the shingles to her.

Mr. Rivera bent over the sawhorses, sawing and measuring. None of us talked.

"Wren!" her mom called from the house. "Come help me, will you?"

Wren looked sideways at me, almost like it was my fault that she had to leave and I didn't.

"Coming!" she called back. She took the glue bottle and brush from me, put them back on the shelf, and left.

Mr. Rivera motioned me over and had me steady a board for him while he clamped it into the vise. "Now you can do this," he said, and handed me a smoothening plane.

It was a little hard to work at first, but then I got the strokes going while he sanded another piece. Whisper-thin curls drifted down onto my sneakers.

"Wren must hate me."

I didn't really mean to say that out loud.

Mr. Rivera stopped sanding and rested his square hands on the board.

"Parker, Wren could never hate you. I think she doesn't understand what's happening. With her friend."

"Well that makes two of us," I said.

Smiling only with his eyes, Wren's dad held up three fingers.

"I tell her don't worry," he said. "Things work out. I tell her you're a good boy."

He went back to sanding, and I listened to the grains rubbing across the wood. Would things work out? If Mr. Rivera knew everything that had been going on, would he be so sure I was a good boy?

I picked up the plane again and tried to focus on the clean feel of wood until the shop clock told me I was way overdue for supper.

Mom got home late that day herself, with things on her mind, so she didn't notice.

"Sorry, Parker," she said. "Dr. Mann's office called. He has to go out of town on Monday, after all. He can't see us until the following week.

Us?

"What a pity," Drog said.

"His receptionist offered to refer us to someone else if it was urgent, but since you got along so well with Dr. Mann . . . Parker, I don't know what to do."

"Don't worry, Mom. I'll be okay, really."

She sighed. "I've heard that before, haven't I? Oh, by the way, here's your *Rubaiyat*."

She pulled the book out of her bag, dusted it off with her sleeve, and handed it to me.

I went up to my room, climbed up the drawer handles to my ledge, and curled up with it while Mom fixed supper.

"Don't bother to read that," Drog said. "Dreadfully boring." He immediately took a nap. Or pretended to.

True, *The Rubaiyat of Omar Khayyam* was hard to get into at first, with all these old-time words like "methought" and "perplext" and names I couldn't even try to pronounce. But after a while I started to catch the rhythm, and some of the lines sounded great, like, "A hair perhaps divides the False and True," or "I came like Water, and like Wind I go" or "There was a Door to which I found no key: There was a veil past which I could not see."

I couldn't tell what the whole thing was about, though. There was a lot in it about drinking wine and about clay pots, and plenty of dust-to-dust stuff, like in the Bible. "Ruby" was mentioned once, but only to describe the color of the wine.

"Not one word about a yacht, Drog," I said, but he just snored.

I was lying around my room on Sunday, practicing lame apologies to Wade Hunt out loud, when Mom called me to the phone. Guess who.

"What's wrong with your mother?"

"I don't know, Dad. She's probably just upset about me."

Dad cleared his throat. "Look, Parker, I've been thinking. Maybe we need to spend more time together."

Brilliant.

"Parker? You still there?"

"Uh-huh."

"Why don't you come for Christmas?"

I considered that for a minute. "Why don't *you*, Dad?"

He sighed. "Son, you know I have another family to think about now."

"Yeah." *Think about your family.*

"Well? I'd really like to have you here."

"What about Mom? She'd be alone then."

"That's true. But I'm sure your mother can take care of herself for one Christmas."

Easy for you to say. Dad never did understand about Mom and Christmas. Why she sticks pine branches in baskets all around the living room and dining room until the house smells like a forest and spends a whole afternoon hanging her collection of ornaments on the tree. Why she always wants us to curl up together on the couch on Christmas Eve to read that famous ghost story, *A Christmas Carol.*

What would Christmas be like at his house?

"I don't know," I said.

"Well, there's still time. Think about it, will you?"

I said I would. But first I had to think about apologizing. How could I ever make myself do it?

Man, I thought. *Everything was fine—well, mostly—before Drog came along. I did okay in school, got along with everybody, made all kinds of things and had fun doing it.* Why couldn't everything just be like it was before?

Well because it can't, that's why, I answered myself. *Drog did happen. He's on your hand, and it doesn't look like he's coming off soon. So now what? What do you want now?*

I wanted to be back in the dojo with Big Boy and Wren at least, and have Sensei be friendly again.

Then apologize and let yourself look weak if you have to. Just because you look weak doesn't mean you are weak, in fact—

That was it! I laughed out loud.

"What?" Drog said.

"I just realized something, Drog. Fighting is easy. Especially if you're mad. What takes guts is to apologize, to let yourself look dumb to someone you were mad with. To be the only one who knows you're not weak for doing that, but strong. Well maybe not the only one. Sensei would know."

"That, dear boy, sounds like advanced dodo-think."

I pocketed him.

"Until," Sensei had said—not "unless"—"Do not speak to me *until* you have done this." That meant he already believed I was strong enough. That I would do it.

I could hardly wait to get it over with.

I had my chance on Monday, which turned out to be my best day in quite a while, starting with some fun I had waking Drog up. I pulled out the Omar Khayyam book and read the first verse to him over his snoring:

195

Wake! For the Sun, who scattered into flight
The Stars before him in the Field of Night,
Drives Night along with the Heavens, and strikes
The Sultan's Turret with a Shaft of Light . . .

"Wh— *What* in the world, Boy . . . ?"

"Drog!" I said. You mean you don't recognize that? It's from the Ruby Yacht!"

He didn't speak to me for hours.

Charlie handed me a note at lunch recess. "Wade Hunt came over to my house yesterday. He told me to give you this."

From the half-scared, half-excited looks on their faces, I could tell his friends already knew what the note said.

Mop Head—
    Meet me at the schoolyard at 5. I dare you. No weapons. Have your friends bring a stretcher. Your going to need it.
                      Wade Hunt

I folded the note and put it in my pocket.

"You're going, right?" Charlie said.

"Can't. I've got aikido practice at five."

"But what about Wade? Parker, you have to!"

"Maybe I'll go to his house instead. A little early."

"Cool, can I come with you?" asked Charlie.

"Me too!"

"Me too!"

"Uh-uh. Just tell me where he lives. I have to do this by myself."

"Our hero," Drog said. "May the farce be with you."

chapter twenty-five

At Wade's, I could see scraps of toilet paper still stuck in the bushes like bits of snow. Wade and his friends were out front throwing rocks, trying to knock down a stack of soda cans, and laughing.

"Here we go, Drog," I whispered.

"Speak for yourself!"

"Hey, Wade . . ." I called out.

He turned around. Wow, his eye! He had what Dad would call a shiner. You couldn't call it a black eye, really, because it was kind of green and yellow.

"You! What're you doing here?" he said. "I told you to meet me at the school."

I walked up to him, ignoring the others and the rocks still in their hands. "I came to apologize. For attacking you the other day."

Wade snickered. "Apologize? Why? Your mommy make you?"

His friends fake-laughed.

Keep your intention, Parker. "I'm sorry I hit you. Sorry about your eye."

"Sorry? I'll make you sorry!" He shoved me to the ground.

I rolled and came up. He lunged at me again and I turned to the side. I could have used his weight to throw him, but I didn't.

"I don't blame you for being mad," I said.

That just made him madder. He reached out for my neck. I ducked and rolled, and he staggered forward.

"Fight back, you puppet freak! Only one of us can be the Man."

"Right, and that's you."

"Huh? You're too weird, you know that?"

"So people tell me."

I laughed then, but not at him. I laughed because taking the one-down position wasn't as hard as I thought. The hard part was deciding to. The hard part was over.

"C'mon," Wade said to the others. "This guy's wasting our time."

They started up the steps. Then Wade turned and said, "I don't get it, Mop Head. You're not scared, but you won't fight."

"I didn't say I wasn't scared. You're pretty tough."

"Yeah, well. How'd you ever learn to fall like that, anyway?"

"I take aikido."

"Aikido?"

"No!" screamed Drog. "You are *not* going to invite this bruiser to aikido!"

"Whoa, Drog! That's a great idea. Wade, you want to come to practice and learn how? You've got nothing to do at five now, right?"

"I—"

"Come here, let me show you something."

He came. Like he was approaching a snake.

"In aikido, if you pushed somebody the way you did me," I said, "he would take hold of your wrists and turn you so both of you are facing the same way, like this. But then he'd throw you. When I throw you to the ground, as soon as you feel yourself going down, duck your head and roll over your shoulder. Ready?"

"Is this some kind of trick?"

I glanced at his friends. "I dare you."

He had to do it.

He landed kind of hard and came up panting, but he got the angle right.

"So . . . why didn't you throw me . . . before?"

"I was giving you a chance to get even. Throw me."

He did and I rolled.

"Come to practice, why don't you?" I said. "It's where the furniture store used to be. The first time is free."

Drog groaned. "First the torcher, now the bone-cruncher!"

"What about that?" Wade said, pointing to Drog. "You practice with that thing on?"

"Yeah."

"So with your mouth you say come to this aikido, but with your hand you say don't, huh?"

I put Drog away. "Don't listen to my hand," I said.

I didn't think he'd show up, but he did.

"Sensei, this is Wade. My used-to-be enemy," I said.

"Jeez," Wade said.

"My sentiments exactly," Drog grumbled into my sleeve.

But Sensei smiled big at me and nodded. "Welcome, Wade. We're just about to warm up."

Then he bowed to me. Long and low. I bowed back even lower.

I felt sure Sensei would have me work with Wade that night, but he paired himself with Wade and Wren with me. I tried to get Wren to fall with me the way she did with Sensei. But she couldn't seem to do it.

When my turn came, I discovered something else she was afraid of. She didn't like to attack. She didn't understand that when you attack in aikido, you're helping each other get better at defense.

I was glad Sensei worked with Wade, though, because he was trying to be a powerhouse before he knew anything, and he could hurt himself. I saw Sensei holding his arms, showing him the motions over and over.

"Going to sign up?" I asked Wade after practice.

"Nah. I thought I'd learn how to fight better, you know, maybe some cool spin-kicks or something? I don't want to learn how to get *out* of a fight, so I guess this aikido stuff's not for me."

"Well, maybe not."

"I know one thing, though. I'm not fighting you anymore. No sense!"

Walking home, I felt light and easy for a change. I had stood up to Wade in a way he didn't expect, and that actually made a bad situation better. He and I sort of respected each other now. Best of all, I made Sensei proud and glad to have me back. Not bad for one day!

chapter twenty-six

Wren and Big Boy and me together again at the dojo, that was something. I got my progress certificate, and one night Sensei invited us all to a special aikido retreat in December. It was going to be a kind of marathon practice from five o'clock to midnight, with students of different levels participating. We had to get our parents' permission.

He said he wanted us to think hard about it too, because he was planning to turn off the heat at the beginning, and the dojo would get colder the longer we practiced. We would wear only our *gi*.

I guess we looked pretty surprised, so he explained.

"In the dojo where I trained in Japan, it was the tradition once a year to break the ice in the river and go for a dip, with only our aikido to keep us warm. It wasn't a stunt. Once you know you can be that cold and overcome it, you don't have to be afraid of any discomfort that comes your way. It makes you feel free."

"Cool," Big Boy said, and we all laughed.

"Ha! That's nothing," Drog said as we left. "You don't know what cold is until you've spent a night in the desert. In the emir's camp—"

"Shhhh, Drog," I said and nudged Big Boy. "Look across the street, in front of the shoe repair shop, but pretend you're not looking."

Big Boy turned back to me and nodded. Notebook Man.

"I see him too," Wren whispered. "Weird. What's he doing here?"

Big Boy and I decided it was time to check this guy out. We hung around after school the next day and sure enough, Notebook Man showed up and followed us.

"Let's lose him," I said.

"Walk slow up the block," Big Boy said. "When we get to Don's Donuts, duck inside. I know a way out the back."

Just before the donut shop, I turned around, looked straight at Notebook Man, and waved my Drog hand at him so that he had to look away and pretend he didn't see. And then he didn't, because we were gone.

The back door of the shop opened out into a cement area with dumpsters and a fence. Big Boy scrambled over the fence and I followed. After a few minutes, Big Boy peeked up over the fence, then ducked down again.

"He's out front, looking up and down the street. He's about to give up."

"Let's see where he goes," I said.

We had fun tailing him for a change. He kept checking his watch and peering around him but not behind, so it was easy to keep him in sight. We ended up in front of Walgreen's, near where we started. He went over and threw his notebook into the back seat of a rusted white Toyota.

"Wow," Drog said. "The magazine business must not pay very well."

Notebook Man leaned against his car and lit a cigarette. Then he took a phone out of his pocket and punched a number. "It's me, Denny. You called me?"

We looked at each other. *Denny?*

"Well, I couldn't until now. . . . So how are you doing?"

He held the phone away from him for a minute and we could hear a scratchy voice on the other end, then he cradled the phone back to his ear with his shoulder and retied his shoe.

"Mom, I'm real busy, you know? Well, sort of a story, but it's a lot bigger than that. This could be it . . . I know, but this is different. . . . It will, Mom, you'll see. Look, don't call me tomorrow, okay? I'll call you . . . Yeah, I promise. Bye now."

"Heaven forbid!" Drog said. "Another mama's boy! Where *do* they all come—"

"Shhh, Drog," I said. Notebook Man had punched another number.

"He's with the big kid," we heard him say. "I lost them for now. What? Because I thought you wanted to know. All right then, whatever you say." He hung up and tossed the phone onto the seat, then he ducked into the store.

Big Boy sprinted toward the car.

"What . . . ?" I said.

He opened the door, grabbed the phone, hit redial, then handed the phone to me.

It rang three times, then a businesslike voice came on: "This is Brian Lockwood . . . Hello? Hello?"

Dad.

I hung up and stared at Big Boy.

"Whooooeee!" Drog said. "The jig is up!"

"Hey!" Notebook Man yelled. What do you think you're doing?"

We jumped.

One-point one-point one-point. "You've . . . been following me," I said.

"Really. Why would I follow you?"

"That's what I'd like to know."

Notebook Man took the phone out of my hand and pocketed it. "You're over your head, kid. Now move, I've got places to go."

"Like to hell, *Denny*?" Drog said. But of course Notebook Man thought that was me.

He smiled, except for his eyes. "You're getting pretty good at that, aren't you? Better watch out." He started the engine.

"Or what," I called after him, "you'll tell my dad?"

"Or you'll end up in a real uniform," he said and roared away from the curb.

"Was I right?" Drog said. "A conspiracy!"

Suddenly I couldn't seem to breathe deep enough. Notebook Man and Dad? A hundred times worse than anything I could have imagined. My own dad had someone spying on me. For what? I wasn't doing anything wrong. Couldn't he trust me? Could I ever trust him now?

We kept glancing behind us on our way to practice, but we didn't see anybody.

"Guess we blew his cover," Big Boy said. He scribbled something and handed me a scrap of paper.

"What's this?"

"The number. I remembered your dad's number from the guy's redial. Thought you might want it."

I swallowed hard. "Wow. That was smart. Thanks." I put the number in my jacket pocket.

How was I ever going to get Mom to believe me about this? Maybe I'd have to have Big Boy come over to back me up.

That turned out not to be a problem, because the minute I walked in the door after practice she said, "Parker, that man you thought was following you. The one you called Notebook Man. What did he look like?"

"He's tall and skinny. Long fingers. Not much hair."

"Does he hold his head a little to the side like this?" she asked.

"That's him! How do you know?"

"He was at the library today, and he was watching me, I'm pretty sure. Writing things down. I went over to ask him why, but he walked out."

"Oh, so you believe me now," I said, louder than I meant to. *Now that you have proof.* "Well, guess what else?"

Mom got panting mad then when I told her about Notebook Man and Dad. She took the phone up to her room and closed the door. She was in there so long I was about to go up and knock, when she came out, looking like she'd run a hard race and come in next to last.

"He promised he would call the guy off," she said. "I wonder if that's because he agrees the whole following thing was wrong, though. Maybe he's just embarrassed about getting caught."

I wondered the same thing.

Mom took a deep breath and let it go.

"At least he apologized. He said the man's name is Dennis. Dennis Masterson. Somebody he went to high school with and knows through business. Apparently when this Dennis mentioned he was going to be writing about your school, Dad asked him to gather some information on your case while he was at it, and then Dennis went beyond that and started following you."

"My case? Dad thinks I'm a *case*?"

"I know. And 'information'! Of course he couldn't have just *discussed* this reasonably, couldn't have just asked me, the one person who's been here all along!"

I could think of someone else who'd been here all along.

Mom ran her hand through her hair. "It's because he has to have *answers*, and the way he sees it, I'm a big part of the problem."

She rolled her shoulders back a couple of times, trying not to heat up again.

"I'm sorry, Parker. Your father should never have done something like this. It was stupid and wrong. But he was probably impatient to help solve your problem."

Well, he was right about one thing. It was *my* problem, not his. And with Notebook Man called off, maybe I'd have one less thing to worry about.

One worry wasn't going away, though. I wasn't any closer to getting Drog off, and Dad must be a lot closer to doing his "something." Notebook Man warned me about a "real uniform," so it didn't take a lot of brains to figure out that "something" was the big B.M.

I'd need ammunition to fight against going, and Dad was already way ahead of me on this. Suddenly I needed to know a lot more about Bradley Military than I could find out on a website. As much as I dreaded it, I had to go back.

I looked up the campus map again on the site, hoping there was another entrance, but no, I would have to walk right up the drive past the Homage to Valor to get to any of the buildings. I checked the bus schedule to make sure I could get out there after school and be back in time for aikido. No matter what happened, I'd need aikido to recover. I stuffed my *gi* into my backpack and wrapped Drog in the bandage.

I must have said *one-point one-point* about sixty times, standing outside the Bradley gate. This time there was a uniformed guy in the sentry box. I made myself go tell him I wanted to talk to someone about coming to Bradley. He looked me over, from my big hair down to my worn sneakers, and asked me if I had an appointment.

Appointment? I said no, I just wanted some information. He asked me my name, got on the phone, and then said Captain Hawkins would see me, just inside the administration building to my right. The gate opened, then closed behind me with a click.

I can only leave here if someone lets me out, I thought.

The sentry pointed to a building right behind the statue. I kept my eyes on my shoes, willing myself not to look up, and managed to get past it.

"So you think you might like to be a Bradley cadet, eh, Parker?" the captain said. "Prospective students normally visit with a parent."

I thought fast. "Um, my father has already contacted you, I think. Sir."

"Oh? Well, let me see." He wheeled his chair over to a filing cabinet and started flipping through the folders. He looked like he must spend his days wheeling around in that chair, because his uniform was pretty tight around the middle. "Lockhart, Lockman . . . ah, here we are. Brian Lockwood, right?"

Until that minute I was still hoping it wasn't true. I nodded.

"Sure enough, your dad requested brochures and an application. Well, I suppose we could show you around, since you're here." He closed the file drawer. "Tell me Parker, do you know any of our cadets?"

"Just Wade Hunt."

One eyebrow rose. "*Just* Wade Hunt," he repeated, mostly to himself. Then he picked up the phone. "Tell Cadet Hunt he's excused from parade and is to report to my office to give a tour of campus."

Captain Hawkins hung up and nodded toward the Ace bandage. "What did you do to your hand? You play sports?"

I couldn't think what to answer, but Wade showed up just in time so I didn't have to.

Wade in uniform, saluting, was an amazing sight—clean and sharp and huge. And he did a huge double take when he saw who he was going to be showing around, but he managed to hold that in until we got outside.

"You! At Bradley? You serious?"

"I might be."

We passed a group of cadets marching, and it seemed like the main reason some of them faced straight ahead was to avoid looking at Wade.

But most of the guys we saw were in sweats, heading for the football field.

"Rec time," Wade explained.

He jutted his chin toward my bandaged hand. "Is that what I think it is? That could be big trouble here."

"It's big trouble everywhere," I said.

"For sure you would have to fight over it. You know how, right?"

I swallowed. "Is there a lot of fighting here?"

"No fighting whatsoever. Strictly against the rules," he said, mock-serious. "So nobody tells."

He stopped in front of an old bluish stone building with small windows. "Well, this is Whitman Hall. Used to be the one classroom building for the whole school. In the basement—"

"Wade, what's it like here?"

"You want the tour or you want to talk?"

"Talk."

He led me to the fourth-year students' barracks. His room had cement-block walls, a cot, a big wooden cupboard, and a dark red curtain over the one window at the end. The desk was a plank fastened to the wall, and couple of board shelves above that held a clock, a radio, a few schoolbooks and a family picture. That was it. A cell.

He noticed me looking around. "We're not supposed to keep much in our rooms, but you wouldn't want to anyway because you've got to clean them spotless for inspection first thing every morning. First-years have inspection twice a day."

"What do you do the rest of the time?" I said.

He motioned me to a folding metal chair and he sat on the cot.

"We march, like you saw. It's called parade. Funny, huh? We go to classes, play sports—everybody has to play at least two sports—eat, study, count our merits and demerits, go to bed. Then get up and do it again. Oh, and third- and fourth-years can get town leave a couple of afternoons a week, on good behavior. In uniform for everything but sports and bed and town leave."

"What classes to they teach?"

"Oh the usual stuff, plus military history. That's required." He leaned forward. "Hey, you're not one of those guys who takes piano lessons or ceramics, are you?"

"I don't take anything except aikido. I like to draw, though."

He lay back on his cot with his feet hanging down off the end. "Well you probably want to keep quiet about that. Sure, they have art and music classes here. The brass just loves guys who go for that stuff, at least on open-house day. So they can show off and say 'See? We got a well-rounded program here, not like you think.'"

"But?"

"But it won't make you points with the guys who really run this place. We have our own demerit system."

"Wade, do the older cadets really torture the first-years at night?"

"If I answer that, will it change your plans one way or the other?"

"Not really."

"Then let's just say if you come here, you're going to need friends."

A bugle call blared from a loudspeaker just outside the barracks. Wade sat up. "Gotta go," he said. "Unless you want to stay for third mess. But the food is something else you don't want to know about until you have to."

He walked with me out to the entrance, saluted the sentry, and before I knew it the gate clicked shut behind me. Then I realized I had just walked by Homage to Valor again with Wade without even thinking about it. I could feel that eagle stare between my shoulder blades, though. I resisted turning back to look, didn't want to push my luck. I saw the bus coming and ran to catch it.

So that was Bradley. Lucky I knew Wade and he was at least friendly enough to tell me what going there would be like. Not as bad as I thought. It was so much worse. I'd be locked in, busy, and bored all day, scared all night. A prisoner. How could Dad want that for me?

chapter twenty-seven

At practice, Sensei talked to us about circles.

"When someone attacks you, turn the attack into a circle. Move toward your opponent rather than away, because often that's where the safe place is for you and for him, the place from which you can turn him. Be aware tonight of the way aikido moves in circles."

"Finally, he admits it," Drog said. "He wants you going around in circles."

Sensei demonstrated the new attack and response, then he paired us. Himself with Wren, Big Boy with me.

I hadn't practiced with Big Boy for a while because Sensei had been putting him with more advanced students, and now I could see why. I tried to think about circles like Sensei said, but really, all I had to do was follow Big Boy and I could just feel them. As big as he was, Big Boy wasn't clumsy at all doing aikido. He was getting good. Whether he attacked or turned or rolled, he was smooth and relaxed. It was like the air around him was water and he was a dolphin or a seal playing and turning in it. And when I practiced with him I felt the same way. I wanted to practice forever.

The two of us walked out of the dojo together.

"Thanks, Big Boy," I said. "That was great." Without thinking, I bowed to him.

He grinned and bowed back. "Hey, man. You got me into this."

We gave each other high fives, then Big Boy got on his bike. He offered me a ride, but I said I wanted to walk.

"'Thanks, Big Boy. Thank you, Sensei,'" Drog said, mocking me. "If you love aikido so much, you ought to say, 'Thank you, Drog.' After all, it's only because of me that you got into it at all."

I was about to say "What?! I do aikido in *spite* of you," when I realized something. How did I happen to be at the Y the day I met Sensei? I went there to pretend to sign up for boxing. Because Dad was upset that I had Drog on my hand. In a way it *was* because of Drog! I had to laugh.

"Okay, Drog, you win," I said. "Thanks for getting me into aikido."

"Ha! Don't you just hate it when I'm right?"

I still felt warm from practice, even though it was December. I unzipped my jacket and stopped to check out a store-window display as I walked through downtown. Three weeks until Christmas, and I hadn't even thought about a present for Mom. Or even what I wanted myself. Pretty soon I'd have to take the bus out to the mall to have a look.

I heard a car pull up behind me and brake. I turned.

The white Toyota. Notebook Man? But Dad promised . . .

I took off, cutting through the block and then doubling back, dodging into doorways until I was sure the white Toyota was nowhere in sight. Then I ran a couple more blocks until I realized where I was going. Ferrisburg Salvage and Iron.

"No!" Drog said as we got to the chained-off driveway. "*What* are you thinking?"

"It's a good place to hide."

But even as I said it I wasn't sure. Except for the boxcar's silhouette a little way in, the junkyard in the dark looked like a strange, broken-up puzzle, a bad-dream scene. Things I couldn't name poked up at crazy angles, and the popped-up hoods of cars seemed to yawn and chomp at me.

Just then a car came around the corner, and I caught a glimpse of light color, maybe white. I jumped over the driveway chain, half-tripping on it, and scrunched down. Remembering something I heard about hiding in the dark, I looked down so no light could catch the whites of my eyes.

The car crawled by. I waited. Waited some more. Then I unbent and peered out into the street. It was empty.

The boxcar. I started picking my way over there through the shadows, but suddenly, *ka-blong! ba-jing!*— a pile of pipes shifted and tumbled to the ground a few feet away. And screamed.

Whooosh! One yowling flash of fur and then another one shot over my feet and landed in the dirt. Two cats rolling over each other, clawing, screeching, biting, trying to turn each other into bloody trash.

I could have sworn I heard Drog mutter "spot-one, spot-one."

I picked up the nearest loose thing, a can, and threw it at the cats, who split apart and scattered, growling low warnings to each other.

"Jeez, Drog. This place is a spook house at night."

"Tell me about it!" he said. "It was the cats I hated most of all."

Right, I forgot. Drog spent a lot of nights in here. Alone.

The light from the streetlamp barely reached us now, and I had to feel my way, risking grabbing or stubbing my toe on something sharp or rusted out. Or worse.

What if the boxcar was. . . occupied?

I came up to it and was about to peek in when I heard shuffling noises. I flattened myself against the side of the car and held my breath, which wasn't easy because I had just finished breathing out.

Slowly a big-eyed face peeked out and around the corner at me.

"Eeeeeyow!" I yelled, and a small body dived spread-eagle out the door, landed on the bed of a nearby truck, then scrambled off and away. My mind formed the word *raccoon*.

"What did I tell you?" Drog said. "A bloody demon-zoo!"

I called into the box car, "Hel . . . Hello?"

No answer. No noise either, so I climbed up and sat in the doorway looking out, breathing out little fog-puffs into the cold.

"No!" Drog said. "Now that you've proven how brave you are, we need to leave. I insist!"

"But what about the white Toyota?"

"What about it? Why should you run from that over-grown Denny punk, anyway? You could take him."

"Drog, you heard what he said about a real uniform. You think Dad can really put me in B.M. if I don't want to go?"

"Hmmmm . . . not if he can't find you. Why not fool everybody and kidnap yourself? That's it! Go where *no* one will think to look. Now if this thing had wheels—"

"But I'm only eleven years old."

"Humph! Where I come from, an eleven-year-old boy is more than old enough to live by his wits. Did I ever tell you about—"

"Where *do* you come from, Drog? I think I have a right to know!" Suddenly I felt like the answer to that must be the key to everything.

"You ask a tough question, Boy."

"Have you really been to the courts of all those emirs and sultans and things?"

"Been to Canton, tra la!"

"China?"

"Ohio. Fooled you, didn't I? Ha-ha!"

I wasn't laughing. I held my Drog hand up to my face and stared right into his eyes.

"NO MORE STORIES, Drog! Don't say another word to me until you answer me. Who ARE you, and how DO you talk? Are you from . . . hell?"

"Ho! You flatter me. Purgatory, more likely."

Whatever that meant, it wasn't an answer. I glared at him.

He sighed. "The truth? Oh, all right, I'll tell you, but you won't like it. You're not the only boy I belonged to, you know."

"You mean the emir's son?"

"No, the boy from Canton, Ohio. What an irresponsible lout. Borrowed me from a playmate and didn't return me when he moved here. Can't recall much about the playmate, but there was a girl before that who lived out in the country somewhere and had nobody to talk to but me. She even sang to me and read to me from her favorite books. Maybe that's when I first learned to talk, at least to myself. I really couldn't say. You see? Not much to go on."

It sounded like another story. "Why should I believe you?"

"Suit yourself. If you ask me, whens and whences are beside the point anyway. All I know is, I seem to end up where I'm needed."

"Where you're NEEDed! Oh, right!" I took a deep breath, not to calm myself, but to fuel up.

"I suppose I NEEDed to lose my left hand and my best friend and have everybody I know think I'm weird or crazy. I NEEDed to get my mom all worried and arguing with Dad. I NEEDed to have Dad send a spy after me and sign me up for military school. And I suppose I NEEDed to give up everything I want to do just so I could be taken over by the world's ugliest, freakiest whatever-you-are!"

"You suppose? Mirror, mirror on the wall, who is the freakiest—"

"YOU'RE the one who's crazy, Drog. I needed you like I needed . . . a case of TOTAL BODY GANGRENE!"

"You might want to stop shouting, Boy. Aren't we supposed to be hiding out?"

"I'll yell if I WANT to," I said, quieting down a little. "YOU were the one who needed ME. Without me, you'd still be rotting in that trash can!"

"Hmmm. I resemble that remark."

Then I realized what I had just said, and it gave me a thought I didn't want to think. Drog didn't choose me. He couldn't. I was the one who insisted on bringing him home. What was that all about? Of course I had no way of knowing what would happen, but still . . .

"Anyway, here we are," he said.

Right. In the junkyard. Freezing.

". . . and for what it's worth, I'm with you on the B.M. question. You must avoid landing in the Big B.M. at all costs."

Those words sent such a jolt of energy and hope through me that even Drog jumped.

"Do you mean that?" I said, cracking a grin. "Then just go limp right now and let me take you off, and presto! This whole nightmare will be history!"

"Ah, not so fast, kiddo. *I'd* be history, you mean. You'd throw me in the trash quicker than—"

"No, I wouldn't, Drog. I promise. Please!"

"You mean to tell me you'd keep me around even if you had a choice? You'd put me back on your hand sometimes to talk? You wouldn't. Not ever."

He had me there. I couldn't even pretend I would.

"You see? Drog knows."

He didn't say that in his usual superior way. More just matter-of-fact and sad.

In spite of myself I felt awful for him then, because it hit me: what must it be like to have no idea who or what you are or where you came—

"Save your pity," he said.

Oh great, was he reading my mind now?

"At least I have my voice," he said. "Take it from Drog, you're nothing without a voice. *Nada.* All that time I lived with Ohio Boy, I kept my thoughts to myself, like you do, and look where that landed me—staring out of a trash can day and night, rain or shine, in a place like a graveyard with no one coming. I swore if I ever got out of there I would have a lot to say about where I go and what I do. Which reminds me. You *know* Drog loathes junkyards, especially at night."

"You're right, Drog, we can't stay here. But I can't go home. Not yet. I have to think. And what if Notebook Man is watching the house?"

"Back to the domo?"

"The dojo. It'll be locked up by now. But maybe . . ."

Would Sensei be mad? I wondered. I had to take the chance.

chapter twenty-eight

I went around in back of the dojo and up the outside stairs that led to Sensei's apartment. I kept hesitating, but my Drog hand reached up and knocked for me.

The door opened right away, as though Sensei had been standing there, waiting.

"Sensei, I . . . I need a place—"

He looked me over and nodded. "You are here," he said.

"It's about my dad—"

"Come in."

I took off my jacket and shoes just inside the door. Sensei's apartment reminded me of the dojo. It did have some furniture, but not much. There was a feeling of space and everything belonging. I calmed down just being there.

"Please," said Sensei. He motioned me over to a corner of the room that had a square of straw mats on the floor and two floor pillows. "I was about to have some tea. Will you join me?"

Mom drinks tea at the kitchen table with Nicole. I tried it once and couldn't see much to like about it. But right then it sounded like just what I wanted. I sat on one of the pillows.

Sensei knelt on the other one. He took two rough brown bowls from a small chest and set them down on the mat as carefully as if they were jewels. He tapped some light green powder into each bowl with a little scooper, then lifted the lid of an iron pot, dipped a wooden ladle into the steaming water, and poured a ladleful slowly into one bowl. He shook a small bamboo whisk back and forth in the bowl until the liquid got all foamy, then he turned the bowl around in his hands, placed it on the mat in front of me, bowed, and said something like *doze-o*. He made another bowl for himself and nodded for us to drink.

Green tea? Tea from a bowl you hold in your hands? I lifted the bowl to my mouth, but before I could taste it, the bright green smell surrounded me. Like grass in the sunshine after a summer rain. And it tasted wonderful.

Sensei put down his bowl. "There is always time for tea," he said. "Now tell me, what's troubling you?"

I set my bowl down too and told him my dad didn't seem to think Mom was doing a good job taking care of me, and he wanted me to go away to military school.

"What am I going to do, Sensei?"

"Yes, of course, that is the question. Parker, you are how old?"

"Eleven. Almost eleven and a half."

"Eleven and a half. At your age, other people are responsible for deciding where you will live and go to school. You don't control your circumstances. But you do control your center. If you strengthen your center, you will be all right wherever you are."

"Even . . . in military school?"

He picked up one of the tea bowls and gazed at it. "Yes."

"This bowl is old. It comes from the Mount Takatori area of Japan. Like every tea bowl, it has a most beautiful side, you see here? You look at the beautiful side while you make the tea, then you turn it toward the guest to serve him. If you like, I will show you how to make this tea sometime."

I nodded.

"Parker, do you know what you want more than anything in the world? Not just this moment but always?"

"I'm not sure."

"If you know what that something is, you will find your strength. In the same way, if you know what your opponent wants most, you can find a way to join him. To lead him."

He began to rinse and wipe the tea bowls. I reached out to help, but he raised his hand. "You are my guest."

He tucked the wiping cloth into his belt.

"Are you ready to let someone know you're here?"

I nodded.

Sensei went over to a low table, scooting on his knees like we do in the dojo, and brought back a phone.

"Mom?"

"Parker! Thank goodness. I was getting worried. Weren't you supposed to—"

"I know. I'm sorry. Mom, listen. It's that Dennis Masterson. I saw him tonight. He's still following me."

"Where are you?!"

"I'm at Sensei's. Upstairs behind the dojo. Can you come get me?"

"I'll be right there!"

"Mom? He's driving an old white Toyota."

While we were waiting for her, Sensei told me he'd been thinking that if we liked doing the upcoming retreat, he would invite members of our class to travel to Japan with him this summer, to a place in the mountains where people from his old dojo hold a retreat every August. We could have fundraisers in the spring to pay for our airfare, and the *aikidoki* in Japan would invite us to stay in their homes and feed us. People who practice aikido are friends all over the world, he said.

Wren and Big Boy and me traveling to Japan? With Sensei? What an amazing thing to think about. If only everything else would just settle down.

Sensei paused a minute and smiled. "In Japan there are some ancient Bunraku puppets that are almost life-sized.

It takes three people to operate each one. Maybe you would like to see them perform?"

"Thank you, no," Drog whispered.

"Do you miss Japan?" I said.

He placed the two tea bowls back in the chest and fastened the latch. "No," he said. "I am happy when I am there, and I am also happy to be here."

Mom knocked on the door, and I went with Sensei to answer.

"Ah, Mrs. Lockwood. From the library! Welcome!" He held out his hand.

"I'm so sorry to impose on you this way," Mom said. "I'm embarrassed."

"No imposition," Sensei replied, "and no need for embarrassment."

Sure enough, she relaxed a bit while I was putting on my shoes. The Sensei effect. Sensei wished us well, said he was confident things would work out.

———

On the way home I told Mom what happened.

She was quiet for a while. The coming-up-with-a-plan kind of quiet I knew better than to interrupt.

Finally she said, "Parker, I'm going to get you a phone. I want you to carry it everywhere. And I'm going to report this."

"Report it? Who to?"

"To the police. We can get a court order to stop Dennis Masterson from following you. And if your father knows anything about this latest incident, he could have some explaining to do, too."

One-point one-point one-point. "Please, Mom, don't get Dad in trouble. Just get me the phone and I'll try to be more . . . aware."

"This should *not* be happening, Parker."

"Mom, I'm so tired. Don't do anything until tomorrow, okay? Talk to Dad first?"

"Oh, I'm definitely going to talk with your father about this!" she said.

No sign of the white Toyota on the way home.

As I undressed for bed, I tried to remember what Mom used to call Dad before he became "your father." I thought they just called each other "Mom" and "Dad" in front of me, but I couldn't be sure.

Drog was tired too, but he was in a good mood. Probably he thought the whole thing was an adventure. He started snoring as soon as we hit the pillow.

chapter twenty-nine

"Oops. We've got mail." Drog was first to notice the fat envelope addressed to Mom sitting on the table in the hall. Unopened. The return address said Bradley Military Academy.

One-point one-point one-point one-point one-point.

I got the milk carton out and put it on the kitchen table, but my hand was shaking too much to pour.

"Mom," I said, "Dad can't make me go to B.M.—er, Bradley Military, can he?"

She sipped her coffee. "No, Parker. Not without my consent."

"You won't give your consent, will you? You can't!"

"Don't worry, Darling. I wasn't planning to."

"But that envelope—"

Mom sighed and set down her coffee cup. "Oh, that. Dad just asked them to send me information. Apparently that fight you got into at school gave him the idea you could hold your own at Bradley."

Now I really felt sick. Before, when I didn't fight, Dad thought I was a wimp who needed to take boxing lessons and go to military school. But when I did fight, that meant I was tough and would fit right in there. I couldn't win.

"He thinks it would be just the thing for you. Says he has his reasons."

"Because I've still got Drog on?"

"That. And because he thinks you'd study harder, and that the academy might make a man out of you."

"But I'm a *boy*, Mom. Can't I just be that for a while?"

"Believe me, Parker, the last thing I want to do is send you off to military school." She stopped buttering her toast for a minute. "But maybe you should tell me why *you* don't want to go. Picture yourself there in the fall. Tell me what you see," she said.

I closed my eyes. My stomach was going up way too fast in a tall elevator and pushing against my throat, just thinking about it. I closed my eyes.

"They've cut off almost all my hair," I said. "When I look in the mirror, I don't see myself. And I can barely breathe in the uniform. Drawing is against the secret rules there, but I'm doing everything I'm supposed to: marching, going to class, playing sports, answering 'Yes, sir!' And everybody's saying it's a good thing. Inside, though, I'm nobody, and I can't go home. I feel like being mean."

"And Drog?" Mom said, almost in a whisper. "Where is he?"

"Well, he's not on my hand. Maybe they did surgery or something. But I can still hear him inside, and he's yelling at me."

Mom pulled me over to her and held on. "Nothing like that is going to happen to you," she said into my hair. "And you will not go to Bradley. Not if I can help it."

The funny thing was, Drog never said a word. Didn't even tell me to quit crying.

Mom told me I could stay home from school that morning because of all that had happened, but I wanted to go. She had to go to work, and I didn't want to be home alone. As I left the house, I heard her calling Dad.

"Brian, you and I need to talk—"

I bolted out the door and down the sidewalk. I felt like I was trying to breathe through a bank of packed gray snow. The whole B.M. thing would probably end in a huge argument. But what could I do?

A long trickle of fear went through me. Fear that I would agree to give B.M. a try, maybe even fake wanting to go, just to keep the peace. Just to keep . . . If I did that, I was pretty sure an iceberg would form inside of me. Not the day I went to B.M., but before. The day I agreed to go.

And if I didn't do it? War between Mom and Dad. If Dad won and sent me to Bradley, Mom would never forgive him and the fighting would never end. But if Mom won out, Dad might just say goodbye and give up being my dad.

If I *chose* to go to Bradley on my own, though, nobody would be the winner, exactly. Dad would be happy and feel like a good dad. Mom would be hurt and lonely and that would be awful. But at least she would try to understand. Mom would never give up on me.

I ran back to the house, grabbed the B.M. envelope, and stuck it inside my jacket.

I saw Wren up ahead walking our old way to school, so I tucked Drog away and hurried to catch up with her. Didn't say anything, just started walking beside her.

"You okay?" she said after a few minutes.

"Got to bed late."

"Oh."

I noticed we were walking exactly in step without trying to. Her energy felt friendly.

"So, do you like aikido now?" I said to keep the feeling going.

She turned to me with shining eyes that just burned that gray snow of mine away.

"Parker, I love it," she said. "All day in school I think about going to the dojo. And I think Sensei is really nice."

We stopped at the corner. "Me too," I said.

"And you know what? I'm getting used to falling. I like it now. It feels like flying."

"Yeah."

We stood there grinning for a while. Then she said she had to go look over her spelling words in case there was a quiz. Good old Wren.

"Well, if you get stuck," I said, "you can always ask your one-point."

She laughed.

Once we got to Mrs. Belcher's room and I slipped into my seat, though, the grayness settled in on me again. I propped up my social studies book so I could open the B.M. envelope behind it. Inside was a booklet for students called "Are You Bradley?" Apparently you were Bradley if you were highly motivated, physically fit, academically excellent, responsible and drug-free, and if you paid attention to detail and always did your best, no excuses. And you had to be a boy. Bradley was one of the few military schools that still didn't give girls an equal chance to be miserable.

You weren't sent to Bradley, you had to *qualify*, and it was a privilege to be accepted. What? The booklet was full of pictures of grinning boys in uniforms and even happier parents with their arms around their sons (what about the *parents'* responsibility?). I knew better, thanks to Wade, but who would believe me?

I stuffed the booklet back in the envelope and put my head down on my desk. Me go to Bradley? There had to be another way.

Everything went back to the impossible. Drog. Drog, Drog. I was going to have to take care of the Drog problem. Fast. Myself. Then maybe everybody would stop worrying about me and getting so drastic. But how? I felt like a train was rushing toward me and my foot was wedged in the track and I couldn't figure out how to get it free.

I kept thinking there was something I needed to consider, something just on the outside edge of my mind that I couldn't quite picture.

Then, right in the middle of social studies, it came to me.

Know what your opponent wants more than anything else, Sensei had said. All this time I'd been thinking about how bad I wanted Drog off and what I could do to get him off. But I never asked myself, what about Drog? Why does he want to stay *on*?

It didn't make sense. He had to be bored hanging out with me, going to bed at ten, to school, to aikido, back home. And he sure didn't stick to me because he liked me.

What if he held onto me because of something worse he *didn't* want?

I waited around after aikido that day. Sensei watched me tie my shoes one-handed, the way I'd I learned to do from a one-armed woman's website, and then stick Drog in my jacket pocket.

"Sensei," I said, "do you think I'll ever solve my puppet problem?"

"I don't know, Parker."

"I mean, it's not just because of Dad and military school. I've been thinking about my hand. It's still in there and I want it back. I want to be able to tie my shoes and make things and throw and fall better in aikido. How can I get my hand back?"

"Parker, I believe you can."

"But how?"

"Until you know, no one knows."

"Then why do you think I can?"

"Because before you just wanted to get rid of Drog. Now you want your hand back."

"Same thing."

"Is it?"

"Please don't make me think, Sensei. Just tell me what to do."

"Practice, Parker. Center yourself and practice. That's the only thing I know."

That night Mom gave me my new phone with her number preset.

"The good news is your dad didn't have anything to do with that business last night," she said. "You're absolutely sure you saw Dennis Masterson downtown . . . ?"

I realized then that I hadn't actually seen him, I ran so fast. "I saw the white Toyota," I said.

". . . because your dad said he spoke to Dennis early in

the evening. In Moline. So that probably wasn't him."

"Oh."

"He also said he's sorry he ever got Dennis involved in the first place. He made it sound like the whole thing was mostly Dennis's idea from the beginning and things just got way out of hand. Does that seem likely? Can you believe your father would let anyone talk him into doing something he thought was a bad idea?"

"Maybe, Mom," I said. Before Drog I would have said no. But what about the Titanium Club? I never would have gone there on my own. "Maybe."

She studied me for quite a while. I didn't look away.

"Well, anyway, he says he's sure Dennis won't bother us anymore. Oh, and he hasn't actually applied to Bradley for you."

Not yet, anyway. Whew.

"Ask her the bad news," Drog said.

Mom closed her eyes. "The bad news is that he wants to review our custody arrangement after Christmas."

"Oh." *One-point one-point one-point.*

"*What for*, Parker?" she said, but she wasn't really talking to me. "Custody? If he wants more time with you, I'm all for that and he knows it. He can come see you any time as it is, but does he? If you ask me, he just wants to make anything that's happened when he's not around officially my fault. Well, I hope his socks rot!"

"Mom!"

She put her hand to her mouth. "I'm sorry, Parker. You shouldn't have to listen to that. Please don't worry—things will work out."

Custody. I wasn't even going to think about it. Out of my control.

PART IV

The False and True

chapter thirty

I had forgotten what Dr. Mann looked like, exactly. It was as though he could look different at different times. I concentrated on memorizing him, drawing him in my mind, and then I said something I didn't mean to say.

"Do you have any kids, Dr. Mann?"

He looked at me. "No, Parker, I don't."

"How come?"

He blinked in surprise. "I—"

My face got hot. *Stupid.* "I'm sorry. I shouldn't have asked that—"

He rested his hand on my arm. "Yes, Parker. Yes, you should. I told you you could say anything you want here. It's just . . . I wanted children very much, but it didn't work out that way. My patients are my only children."

Then I told him about the picture of Dad and me sledding. I asked him if he thought I was right about that.

"Parker, I'm sure he loved you once. But unless I miss my guess, he never stopped."

"But if he loves me, wouldn't he want to be with me? Why would he want to send me away to military school where I could only come home once in a while? What kind of love is that?"

Dr. Mann nodded. "Complicated, I'm sure," he said. "Let me guess some more. He probably thinks the school would give you male examples you don't have with him away, and help you grow up strong. He is probably hoping you'll understand when you're older and thank him."

"He doesn't know me. He doesn't understand how I feel."

"I'm sure that's true. Have you told him?"

Suddenly I felt so heavy I wanted to fall asleep right there in the chair.

"I'm really tired," I said.

"I'll bet you are, Parker. You accomplished something important today."

"I did? What?"

"You asked me a direct question that I had to answer."

"About kids, you mean?"

"Yes. Questions like that can be a good way to clear things up, even if they make people uncomfortable at first. Just put your thoughts or questions out there, tell or ask for the truth, and see what happens."

"Even with my dad?"

"Perhaps especially with your dad."

"Hmmm," Drog said. "Did hell just freeze over?"

All I could think about at school was that I needed to figure out something about Drog. Okay, what *doesn't* he want? I asked myself. What's he afraid of? Trash cans. Being thrown away, forgotten. Drog is afraid of being . . . nobody.

So what does he do about that? Whoa, wait a minute! Drog can't *do* anything. He has hands, but he can't operate them himself. I'd hate that. Worse even than not being able to walk. The only thing Drog can do is talk. So he bosses and insults people all day long. In a weird way, that makes him somebody, because you can't ignore him. As long as Drog can stay on my hand, give me a hard time, and get me to answer, he won't be nobody.

Math quiz. I completely forgot. I let Drog figure out how to do the problems while I went on working on the problem of him. Okay. I knew what he didn't want. But what if I could think of something he did want? Something he wanted so bad he'd be willing to leave my hand for it? Wouldn't that be amazing? What if I didn't need to do something *about* Drog? What if I needed to do something *for* him?

"Parker, are you still with us?"

"Uh, no, Mrs. Belcher. Sorry."

"Well, are you planning to join us soon?"

I got out of my seat and walked up to her desk. "I'm thinking about something really important," I said, so only she could hear me. "Could I please just think for a while?"

She sighed. "Parker, I don't think anyone ever asked me that before. And if they did, I don't believe they asked me so nicely."

"Does that mean yes?"

"Yes, Parker. You may go on thinking. As long as you turn in that math quiz first."

I didn't even realize I had it in my hand.

I decided right then that Mrs. Belcher was the best teacher I'd ever had. I went back to my seat and thought.

What did Drog like most? Excitement, but more than that. He liked to stir things up. When had I seen him the happiest? The night he took over the puppet play and turned it upside down. Was it attention he wanted? Applause?

By art period I had it figured out. Drog didn't just need to be a troublemaker, he wanted to be admired for it!

How could I help Drog be good at being bad?

For the first time in a long time, I drew a picture of him. He turned out more like a mischief-maker than a demon.

Wren wasn't around after school, so I walked home by myself, still working out what I was going to do for Drog. What if he could be in another play? One where he was actually supposed to make trouble?

I threw my book bag on my bed, turned on the computer, and googled "puppets." A couple hundred sites came

243

up. Sites for buying puppets and puppet theaters. Sites for Punch-and-Judy puppet makers, mostly in England.

I tried "puppet productions" and found hundreds more sites under that. Most of the puppet troupes put on fairy tales or health-and-safety plays for elementary schools. On the third page of entries I found a site called Preposterous Puppets. I clicked on the contact-us link and typed a message in the box:

> My name is Parker Lockwood. I have this puppet named Drog who loves trouble. He has a smart mouth, he's bossy, and he tells wild stories. I need to find something to keep him busy as soon as possible. Something outrageous. Please give me some advice.

I did some homework, then I turned on the computer again and found a return message from a guy named Sergio at Preposterous Puppets.

> Parker,
> Your Drog character sounds great. We're in Peoria between tours right now. Any chance you could bring him here on Saturday? We'd like to see what this Drog can do. Sergio

I answered, "Okay. I'll ask my mom."

"Your mom? How old are you?"

"Eleven."

"Oh. Hmmmmmm. Well come anyway, if you can. Here's the address."

———————————

"Guess what, Drog?" I said. "You and I are going to Peoria on Saturday for a tryout! There's a puppet troupe there that thinks you sound really interesting."

"You don't say!"

"I do say, Drog. So we're going. If Mom will let us, I mean."

"If Mom will let us? You are hopeless, Boy."

It did take some convincing to get Mom to drive me to Peoria, so soon after the Titanium Club thing, to get together with a puppeteer I just met on the Internet. Especially since I didn't want her to be there for the audition. But we worked it out: she would drive me there, go in and meet Sergio, then go do some shopping and come back. And we would both have our cell phones.

"But let's not tell your father about this, okay?"

Who, me?

"Oh, I forgot to tell you. He called again to apologize, and he really did sound sorry. We talked a little about Christmas. He told me he's sending you something. An early present. Something special."

"He is?" Why didn't he tell *me*?

chapter thirty-one

"Just think, Boy, thanks to me, you're going to Peoria," Drog said.

I laughed. "You're right, Drog. I definitely couldn't have done it without you."

"Saturday Peoria, next week the world!"

"Um. Could be."

What I didn't say to him or even to Mom was that I wasn't trying out for both of us, just Drog. If things went like I planned, I'd come home on Saturday with my hand free, leaving Drog with the troupe. If not . . . well, I was pretty sure it would work. It had to.

For the rest of the week I dreamed about how great it would be to have my hand back. I spent a lot of time in the spare room, running my free hand over the stuff in there and thinking what I might make with it.

Mom and I would get home from Peoria in plenty of time for me to go to the aikido retreat and celebrate. For the first time I let myself imagine the trip to Japan with Sensei and Wren and Big Boy. After Drog was gone, I'd have to talk to Mom about that.

On Wednesday, the package came from Dad. The words on the box read, "The Way Things Work Kit." I couldn't believe it. It was just like *The Way Things Work* book we had in our room at school, except this had all the stuff you needed—dowels, gears—to make everything the book talked about. It was fantastic.

It made me mad. How could Dad know there was such a thing? How could he know I would like it?

It was a lot easier to think of Dad as clueless. Easier than being confused. It was a perfect present. But it would take two hands, and Dad knew that. I still had only one, and for all he knew, I didn't have any plan to get the other one back, so what was he trying to do? I went back to my room, closed the box, and put it up on the shelf over my bed.

Friday morning. With any luck, it would be the last day Drog would be with me at school, so as soon as I got to the playground, I took him out of my pocket.

"Drog, I want you to do me a big favor," I said. "I want you to talk for Wren today. Show her I've been telling the truth."

"Sorry, Boy, no can do. Matter of self-respect."

"Come on, Drog. You have to."

"Nokey-dokey. Talk to her yourself."

What could I say to Wren that I hadn't said a dozen times already?

"Parker? . . . Parker?"

I turned around. It was Wren.

"I heard."

"Heard what?"

"Him. Drog. Talking to you."

The last time she had looked at me so wide-eyed was the day two years ago when I told her Dad was getting married again.

"You didn't know I was behind you, did you?" she said.

I shook my head. "Looks like Drog didn't either."

"So you couldn't have . . . Parker, I am so sorry."

She stared at Drog then like he was a hand-eating monster she was seeing for the first time.

"He's so . . . You must hate me. For thinking you made all this up."

The pain on her face made my throat hurt, and I had to look down for a minute.

"No Wren. I don't hate you."

"But you kept saying believe me, and I didn't. I wish I'd believed you."

"Yeah. Me too."

"I should have tried to help you instead of just getting worried and mad. But I was afraid you—"

"What?"

"That you were going loco or something. Or . . . trying to get rid of me. Or both."

"Get rid of you? That *would* be crazy."

She started a smile, then erased it.

"I just didn't think any of it could be true. About Drog. It still can't. But it is, right?"

"Right."

"You know, it's kind of your fault too, Parker. You didn't believe me either."

"I didn't? About what?"

"The bad feeling I had about the puppet. Right away. I wanted you listen to me, even if you didn't agree. I wanted you to say, 'Okay, if you feel that way, let's leave it.'"

I could see what she meant. "Yeah, I guess I should have. But I didn't, and then everything got —"

Wren pointed at Drog, who was keeping up a steady blank act, and shivered.

"What is he then? How does he talk?"

I shrugged. "I'm not sure even he knows. He just . . . is."

"And you really can't get him off?"

"Nope."

"Well, what are we going to do about him? Have you tried . . . ?"

We? What are *we* going to do about him? I wanted to fly.

"Wren, I've tried a lot of things, but it's not just Drog now. It's Dad. Dad and Mom. I can't explain it all."

She took hold of my hand. "Don't then, Parker. It's okay. Just let me help."

"You are, Wren. You're on my side now!"

That was really all I needed right then, but Wren always needs something to do.

"Maybe you could tell Mom that you heard Drog," I said, "and that you know it was him, not me? She might believe you."

"I will!"

Say it quick. "Wren, I might go to Bradley Military next year."

She jumped back and dropped my hand. "What? No! Parker you can't!"

"I know. But I might. Would you still be on my side, then?"

She took a big breath and let it out. "I would, I promise, but . . . Do you have to go? Is your dad making you?"

"Not exactly. I might have to anyway though, unless—"

"Unless what?"

"Well, I could get real lucky soon." I held my finger to my lips behind Drog's back. "Tomorrow. I'll know tomorrow. Cross your fingers for me?"

She crossed fingers on both of her hands, and then added the ring fingers and pinkies to the crosses until they looked like big triple knots. We both laughed, and before I realized what I was doing, I hugged her. Partly because my eyes were starting to water up and didn't want her to see.

"You idiot!" Drog yelled.

Wren pulled back and looked at me.

"That was Drog," I said. "That was you, wasn't it, Drog?"

He went back to his empty stare thing.

"Wren, he's probably just mad that you found him out."

She laughed, a bubbly kind of laugh I'd never heard from her.

"Uh oh. He'll probably really let me have it now," I said. But I let myself laugh, too, and kept it up no matter how hard Drog squeezed. Pretty soon laughing and crying got all mixed up.

After a while, with just a few more giggly hiccups from Wren, we went up to Mrs. Belcher's room. Wren reached into her jeans pocket pulled out her stone, her maybe-agate, and handed it to me.

"Wren?"

"You need this more than I do," she said. "Keep it for now, okay?"

The rest of the morning we grinned at each other from behind our notebooks, and just before lunch she sent me a note:

I'm pretty sure I'm getting a pet mouse for Christmas. If I do, want to help me build a house for him?

I gave her a thumbs-up with my free hand, then took her stone out of my pocket. It was a little bumpier than I remembered, but creamy-feeling. I set it down on my desk, turned over my social studies worksheet, and sketched Wren holding out the stone to me. It had a little crack in it. Like her smile. For the background, I drew a kind of agate-pattern archway. It was the best Wren drawing I had ever done.

My left hand was pretty sore from all Drog's squeezing, and I couldn't let him stay mad for the audition, so I took him out after school and tried to get him going again.

"Drog?" I said.

Silence.

"Oh, so now you're not talking to *me*."

More silence.

I had to get him talking before Peoria. "How come you called me an idiot this morning?"

He couldn't resist that one.

"If you don't know the answer, that just shows what an idiot you are."

"No, really. Why?"

"Ha! You are an idiot because you don't even know survival rule number two: NEVER TRUST GIRLS!"

Blend with him. "You're right, Drog, I don't know that rule. What's rule number one?"

"What else? TRUST ONLY DROG!"

The rest of that day and evening crawled, so I got down the Way Things Work Kit, took all the pieces out, and read the instructions. It even had directions for making a sail-powered land yacht! Maybe if I got Drog to stay in Peoria, I could make that one and paint it ruby red in memory of him. Maybe, maybe.

The drawings kept giving me more and more ideas of my own. By the time I put the kit back on the shelf, I could see myself building hundreds of things, starting with some hideouts and tunnels and skywalks for Wren's mouse that would turn her whole room into one big mouse playground. *If* I got my hand back.

I lay in bed a long time before falling asleep that night, and it wasn't because of Drog's snoring. I was thinking too much to sleep. Now that I had a pretty good idea what Drog needed, and at least a long-shot plan for what to do about him, what about me? I never did answer Sensei's question. What did I want more than anything? I started this sentence in my mind, *Most of all, I want . . .* I was about to say . . . *my hand to be free . . .* but that didn't sound right. It was really important, but it wasn't enough.

"Not just for now, but always," Sensei had said.

I tried again. *What I want most is . . .*

"What I want most," I said out loud, "is just to be who I am and—"

That woke Drog up.

"Who are you talking to, Boy?" he grumbled. "What time is it, anyway?"

"It's almost midnight, Drog. Go back to sleep."

He soon went back to snoring, and I tried the sentence again, this time in my head.

What I want most is to just be who I am and . . .

Something about other people. What did I want with them? Whatever it was, it was something I almost had with Mom and Sensei and Big Boy and Mrs. Belcher and now Wren again. Almost. And I definitely needed more of it with Dad.

I want the people close to me to . . . what? A word came into my head as if someone said it: *respect*. I wanted respect. What did that mean?

I tried the whole thing again. *I just want to be me. And I want the people close to me to respect me and trust me and believe me. Even if I tell them something that sounds impossible.* Yes! That sounded true. Like something I would want forever. I said it over to memorize it. Then I added something at the end. *I want us to respect and trust each other.*

I got out of bed in slow motion so I wouldn't wake Drog up again, then I took the number Big Boy saved for me out of my jacket, leaned over to the night light, and programmed it into my phone. Maybe I'd have a call to make on Saturday.

When I tunneled back under the covers, though, I realized I was forgetting something. Most of those things I wanted depended on other people wanting them too. What if they didn't? What if people never did quite believe or trust me again without proof, because they couldn't? Or didn't want to? What then? Being myself was the only thing left on my list that I could do on my own. Would I still want to be myself if it meant being . . . alone?

That was way too hard to think about. I closed my eyes and tried to sleep, pushing wood pieces around in my mind. Some of them were egg-shaped, like Wren's stone, and I imagined secret swirls inside of them.

A voice said: "Don't give up, Parker."

I opened my eyes again. Drog was still asleep, so it wasn't him, and there was no one else in the room.

I had said it myself. *Don't give up.*

chapter thirty-two

"Wake up, Boy. You're going to make us late!"

"Wha—" I rolled over and looked at the clock. "Drog, it's only five thirty."

"But I need to rehearse! My entries, my soliloquies, my asides . . ."

"How can you rehearse? We won't even know what they want us to do until we get there."

"Exactly why I must be prepared for anything!" He cleared his throat. "It is a far, far, better thing I do—"

He wasn't going to quit, so I sat up in bed, pulled the blankets around me, and tried to be awake. Then I was, because I started worrying, too. If Drog got too nervous, he might mess up at the audition. *One-point one-point.*

"To be or not to be, that is the question. Whether 'tis nobler—"

"Drog," I said. "They probably just want you to say whatever you think of at the time. So don't worry, just be obnoxious and you'll be great. You're good at that."

"You're right, Boy! I am!"

"So the best thing you could do right now is to save your voice for Peoria."

"Very well then!"

He crooned to himself, "Am I bad? Oh yes!" and then he actually stopped talking. I couldn't believe it. I couldn't get back to sleep, though, so I got dressed in the dark and went downstairs. When Mom finally came down, I gulped my cereal and flopped from the chair to the couch to the chair, waiting for her to get ready in slow motion.

As soon as we backed out of the driveway, though, I started getting pebbles in my stomach. Dad always drove me crazy saying, "If something seems too good to be true, Parker, it probably is." It sure looked like my idea of getting Drog to join a puppet troupe might be one of those too-good things, and I didn't have another plan.

The car was still heating up, so I put my free hand into my other pocket and held Wren's stone. A few snowflakes twirled down to the windshield and melted. Mom tried to make conversation as we drove, but I could only answer "uh-huh."

I was hoping it would take us a while to find the theater, but Mom had good directions and we hit all the green lights. There was even a sign on the front of the theater with an arrow that said, "Parker Lockwood. Please come to the stage door."

Mom tried the handle, then knocked on the stage door. A man in a black T-shirt opened it and smiled at us.

"You must be Parker," he said to me. Come on in."

"And are you Sergio?" Mom asked.

He laughed. "Oh, no, I'm Tony. Sergio's on stage, warming up. Follow me."

I'd never been backstage in a real theater. Everywhere I looked there were tall, tall ladders and long ropes on pulleys and panels of switches. The heavy maroon curtains gave off a wonderful dusty smell.

Except for Sergio, dressed all in black and standing in the middle, the stage was bare, and it was bigger than our whole school cafeteria. It echoed. There was no puppet stage to stand behind, like we had at school. Was I going to have to stand out there by myself?

We waited for Sergio to finish his warm-up. Suddenly the words he was booming out into the theater connected with my brain.

"Would you that spangle of Existence spend
About the Secret—Quick about it, Friend!"

It was from the *Rubaiyat*! And I knew the next line!

"A hair perhaps divides the False and True..." I called out.

Without breaking rhythm, Sergio turned toward me, flashed me the greatest smile I have ever seen in my life, and said,

"Yes. And a single Alif were the clue—
Could you but find it—to the Treasure-house,
And peradventure to the Master too . . ."

For a magic minute nobody moved. Sergio broke the spell.

"The *Rubaiyat!*" he said. "How do you know it, Parker?"

My face got warm, but it wasn't like being embarrassed. I glanced at Mom. Her mouth hung open.

"From Drog, sort of." I said. "It's a long story."

Sergio came over and shook my hand. "Great," he said. "Long stories are the best, don't you think? Glad to meet you."

Sergio introduced himself to Mom. They chatted for a minute, then she told him she had to go do some errands, like we planned. She held up her phone. I showed her mine, and gave her a yes-I-know-Mom look. The door closed behind her with a little wheezing sound.

"So this is Drog," Sergio said, looking him over and smiling "I'll bet he's a character, all right. Where'd you say you got him?"

Drog squeezed me hard, so I just shrugged.

"Well, Parker," Sergio said, "Let's see what you can do."

"Um, I don't actually do anything," I said. "It's Drog talking."

Sergio winked at me. "Right. Well then, Drog, meet Jasmine, the other puppet in this scene. We haven't been able to come up with a good match for her. She doesn't exactly . . . cooperate."

Sergio walked over to a shelf and brought down a super-curvy girl puppet with long black hair, a red mouth, and dangly earrings. And a glittery turquoise costume. I couldn't believe my luck. She looked like a belly dancer!

Sergio slipped the puppet onto his hand.

"Vrrrum, vrrrrum!" Drog said.

Vrrrum, vrrrrum? Jeez, Drog.

"But Sergio," Jasmine said, "you don't expect me to perform with this . . . creature, do you? He's so awfully . . . green."

Drog cleared his throat. "You will call me Drog," he said.

"Drog? Drog? Hmmm. I don't think so," Jasmine said. "Frog, maybe. That has a certain greenness to it."

Oh no. PLEASE don't make fun of his name.

"It's Drog, I say! Show some respect! I was once the right-hand man of an emir!"

"Well that was then, wasn't it?" Jasmine said. "I don't see any emirs around here."

"Fortunately for you!" Drog said. "A girl like you would last less than a day at the emir's court. You'd be a mere momentary distraction."

"And what would you be, a mere *toady*? You've never been in any emir's court. You're pulling my leg."

"I would pull your leg gladly, dear girl, if only you had one."

Amazing. Drog didn't even sound mad. If I called him Frog . . .

Sergio grinned. "Well, I guess that does it for introductions. Keep it up Parker, you're doing great."

"But I—"

"Now you and Drog come over and stand next to me, facing out. Pretend the house is full."

I lined up next to Sergio and peered out into the dark, my stomach quivering.

"Here's the situation. Drog and Jasmine are the last two contestants left in a special kind of talent contest. It's an insult and aggravation competition, and this is the final round."

"*Excelente!*" Drog whispered to me. "How can I not win? Drog, the Master of Insult, the Avatar of Aggravation! Besides, this girl has a fatal weakness—she likes me!"

What? One of my knees started bobbing up and down. I couldn't hold it still.

"Excuse me," Drog said to Sergio. "What's the prize?"

"It's a ticket. On the very first tourist flight to the moon!"

"Whee!" Drog said. "Start measuring me for my spacesuit."

"This is improv," Sergio was saying, "so let's just take it from here."

Drog cleared his throat. "Women and children first."

Sergio grinned at me, snickered, and then shut his eyes. When he opened them again, he was Jasmine.

"Keep in mind, Frog," she said, "I'm an animal trainer in my day job."

"Ah, such a pity. Why can't girls give up trying to compete with men and just be the charming *trinkets* they were born to be?"

Whoa, Drog.

"And why can't frogs stay plopped in their slimy ponds, chomping at flies? You weren't born, even, you were *hatched.*"

Drog answered right back. "Ho! I would my horse had the speed of your tongue—"

"You don't have a horse, Sweetheart, and as a quoter of Shakespeare, you croak."

"You see," Drog whispered to me, "she called me sweetheart. Va-va-voom!"

"Are you still talking, Signior Frog? Nobody marks you."

"Ah, so, you've actually heard of Shakespeare?" Drog said to Jasmine. "You're not as shallow a creature as I thought. This may yet prove an amusing competition."

"Ha! A *losing* competition, you mean—for you. 'A bird of my tongue is better than a beast of yours.'"

"Well done! Unfortunately, the bird of your tongue is a crow. You're a lady definitely not meant to be heard. But seen, yes. After all, there's so much *of* you to see."

"At least *I* have hair. And what's that you're wearing? A lost sock?"

"Well what about you, my udderly bovine beauty? Your curvature's like the earth's—nearly round, that is. Your rolls roll when you rotate. Not that I mind, you understand."

Uh-oh. Was this working?

"I understand you're the big *Rubaiyat* expert," Jasmine said. "So woo me with your best lines, Frog."

Oh no. He doesn't know anything. But before I had a

chance to answer for him, Drog said, "Haven't I met you somewhere before? Do you come here often? What's a naughty girl like you doing in a place like—"

"Not that kind of line!" Jasmine screeched.

"Well, *rolling* right along . . ."

Sergio broke in with an announcer voice, "Time's up, and it looks like we have a tie. That means each of the final contestants gets half the prize."

"Ah" Drog said, "shall we go together halfway and back? At least see some stars?"

"I've got a better idea. You go and I'll come back. What a fool you are, Frog! There's no way to split the prize."

"If you really think I'm a frog, come give me a kiss. Who knows? You might get a prince as reward."

Jasmine put her hands on her hips. "Sometimes a frog is just a *frog*," she said.

"Never know till you try."

"Me kiss you? No way!"

"So, not only a cow, now, but a cowardess! Tell you what. Kiss me and I'll let you win the contest. One kiss, and you'll go to the moon!"

Sergio was trying so hard not to laugh that he could barely be Jasmine.

She covered her eyes with one hand. "Oh well, then," she groaned, "for the prize. Here goes."

She gave Drog a long smack on the mouth. Too long. Yuck. Then she pulled back to look.

"I knew it! You tricked me! You're every bit as green as before."

"You were expecting the moon and a prince, too?" Drog said. "Not every prince is handsome, you know. Some just have . . . beautiful character."

Sergio chuckled.

Jasmine shook her head. "I'll say this for you, Frog. You're one disgustingly good kisser. I don't *want* to like you, but . . . did I just win?"

"You see?" Drog said, "I'm an enchanted prince after all."

Sergio dropped his puppet hand to his side and roared with laughter, then slapped me on the back. "Perfect!" he said.

Yes! My knee wasn't jerking anymore, and I wanted us to go on and on. *Whoa, take it easy, Parker. Keep your intention.*

After all that excitement, I had to find a bathroom. Sergio slipped Jasmine off and pointed me to a door backstage.

"Whooooeee. What fun!" Drog said. "Quite a girl, that Jasmine! No peace and harmony with her, no sireee! And wasn't I bad? Awfully, deliciously bad?"

"Drog, you were so bad you were good." *It's working. It's working.*

"I was, wasn't I?" Drog said, gazing into the bathroom mirror. "Now they'll have to take us into their troupe!"

Us? "Well, maybe."

"What do you mean, maybe? Have some confidence! I have to hand it to you, Boy! You've found us some quality people at last!"

When we came back out, Sergio said, "That was great, Parker. You've got real talent, and we hope you'll join Pre-posterous Puppets, in spite of your age—"

"What did I tell you!" Drog said.

"—but you're going to have to talk it over with your folks. We go on tour a lot and you'd miss some school."

"Thanks, Sergio," I said, "but—I know you'll think I'm weird—it's Drog who has the acting talent. Drog does all the talking. I'm just the hand."

He nodded. "I've been doing this a long time, and I know very well what happens when you put a puppet on. Sure they talk, and you can't always control who they are or what they say. So no, I don't think you're weird. Gets a little spooky sometimes though, doesn't it?"

I nodded. He understood. I had never felt less weird in my life.

"The thing is, this guy's so off the wall we want him in our show. And we're not sure he'd do it without you. Maybe you're . . . the perfect team."

"Right!" Drog said. "So what are you waiting for, Parker? Where do we sign?"

"Excuse us, Sergio, we need to talk."

"Sure."

chapter thirty-three

I stepped into the bright alley and turned Drog so he wouldn't be facing the dumpster.

"Drog! Do you realize you called me by my name in there? You actually called me Parker!"

"Did I? What was I thinking?"

"This troupe's a great thing for you, isn't it?"

"Great? It's brilliant! I'll be witty and wicked and sarcastic, and people will laugh and love me, just like Punch. But I can say whatever I want. Punch had to say the same lines over and over—"

"Great for you, but not so good for me right now. I need to go to school and practice aikido and be with my mom. And my dad."

"But—"

"So what I'm thinking is, since you're such a terrific

puppet and actor all you need is a hand. Any hand. Why don't *you* join the puppet troupe? Sergio understands you. He likes you exactly the way you—"

"No! You heard what he said. You and I, we're the perfect team. You know, I had a great idea in there. You make a Parker puppet for your other hand, dressed in your dodo uniform, and we have a two-man act. I play all the villains and bosses and kings and you play the fall guy. Get it? The fall guy, ha-ha! And of course I always get the girl. We'd be huge."

"No, no, Drog, it's you they want. I'd just hold you back. Go with the troupe."

"Wait a minute," Drog said. "Wait just a blooming minute. Now I get it. Sergio doesn't really need another puppet, does he?"

"What?"

"This is all a plot! A plot to get rid of me! You and your mother and Sergio, you're all in this together aren't you?"

"No, Drog, you don't—"

"And to think I almost took the bait! Well, you don't fool Drog twice. No sirree! I'm sticking with you, no matter what!"

No, no. My one chance.

"Drog, you've got it all wrong. I'm trying to do what's best for you, honest."

"Honest? You? When were you ever honest?"

"What do you mean? I'm honest!"

"Hah! Don't forget, I know you. You like to fight, but you hate to admit it. Yes? You're angry but you pretend you're not. You let people push you out of shape and only talk back to them when you think they can't hear you."

"I—"

"You're a coward pure and simple, Boy, and cowards are never honest. The truth is, you couldn't get along without me!"

"Oh, couldn't I?"

"No, you couldn't. You need Drog for backbone. Look at you, all tied up in knots whenever your mother or your girl-friend doesn't like something you do. You're never going to learn to stand up to people. Especially not that father of yours. When you're forty years old, you'll probably still be saying 'Sorry, Dad. Okay, Dad.' You'll never get him to re-spect you."

My shoulders got tight. "Oh yeah?"

"Yeah, as you would say."

"Well, watch this!"

The vein in my neck started thumping, and my mind sure wasn't on my stomach mole. I whipped out my phone and punched a number. Dad's.

Suddenly that hot, bring-it-on feeling felt awfully familiar. The same feeling I had just before I attacked Wade. The same. I pushed the end-call button before the phone could ring on the other end.

"See what I mean?" Drog said.

I lowered both my Drog hand and my phone hand then and just stood there breathing in-out, in-out for a while.

"Yeah, Drog," I said. "I do see what you mean." I lifted the phone and punched the number again with my thumb, then closed my eyes. *What do I really want to say to my dad? Just between him and me?"*

His phone rang. Rang again.

One-point one-point one-point one.

"Brian Lockwood here."

My eyes opened. "Hello, Dad."

"Wha— Parker? But how did you get this number?"

"From your friend. From Dennis Masterson."

One-point one-point.

"Dad, I know you've been worried about me—"

"Look, Parker, if this is about the other night—"

"I just want to say that if you want to know something, you don't have to have anybody check up on me. You can ask me."

"That was a bad idea I know, Parker. I regret it."

"You scared me, Dad."

"Ah. I didn't mean to do that. I'm sorry." He sighed. "I've been kind of scared myself lately. About you."

Dad? Not just worried, but scared? I believed him. But I had to go on.

"About Bradley Military, Dad—I can't go there. It would be bad for me. The worst."

He was quiet for a minute. "I suppose you're not really a cadet."

"No, I'm not. I'm . . . more of . . . a maker." *At least I was. At least I want to be.* "I like to dream up things, and then make them. Turn nothing into something. Rules and schedules kind of get in my way."

"That's exactly what worries me, Parker. I can't see where any of that is going to take you. I thought Bradley would be good for you in the long run, give you some discipline, you know? An atmosphere where you could focus more, learn how to think."

"I am learning that. Another way. I know you always want me to use my head, but . . . I think with my hands."

As soon as I said that, I realized it was true.

"Hmmmm. Of course with all your drawing and constructing things, you could probably go into architecture or industrial design or . . . I just worry that I ought to be doing something to help you find your way in life."

"Dad, believe me, the best thing you could do for me right now would be to stop worrying about me."

"Okay, I'm listening."

One-point one-point. "Dad? Where have you been?"

There was a long silence then, but I didn't try to fill it up. I wasn't sorry I asked.

I could hear him take a deep breath. And then another one.

"You know," he said, "at first I thought you and I would

spend a lot of time together. But I didn't feel comfortable at the old house anymore. I thought by coming there to visit I'd just give you the idea that your mother and I would get back together. So it had to be at my place. But it was hard to think of enough things to do and talk about with you. I wasn't used to that, Parker, and when it happened, I turned my attention to what I do know. My work. I'm not saying that was right, it's just how it was."

I swallowed. "What about now?"

"I— I've had regrets."

Neither of us spoke for a minute.

"Have you thought any more about Christmas?" he said, finally.

Take a chance, Parker. Say it.

"I'd like to spend Christmas with you, Dad. And Shanna."

"You would? That's wonderful, Parker. That's . . . that's great!"

"We get out of school on the twenty-first."

"Okay! I'll come pick you up. And Parker, if there's enough snow . . . want to go sledding? Just us? Do you still like to do that?"

Sledding. Sledding. The word got all mixed up with the sound of my heart beating, and I couldn't answer for a minute. "Yeah, Dad, I'd like that." I knew then what I wanted for Christmas. Snow. A lot of snow.

"What about . . . will you be bringing—"

"Drog?" I couldn't resist. "Have I told you how good he is in math, Dad?"

"I mean, you can bring him if you have to." Dad sighed. "Just keep him put away, I guess."

"No. I don't have to. I . . . I won't be bringing him."

I expected Drog to crush my hand like a python then, but what I felt was nothing. Nothing.

I lifted my Drog hand, but all I saw was my bare hand.

"Dad! Sorry, I gotta hang up!"

"But—"

"Bye."

I whipped around. There, lying on the cold ground behind my feet, was Drog, or what was left of him. He looked so little. So empty.

chapter thirty-four

"Drog!" I yelled.

No answer.

Exactly what I had been praying for: Drog off my hand. Free at last. But it was all wrong. I didn't want him to just . . . end.

I plucked him up by the head and shoulders and ran back into the auditorium.

"Whoa," Sergio said, "what's the hurry?"

"It's . . . I've decided. Drog will join the troupe without me. Could you put him on, quick?"

"Sure." He reached out and took Drog from me.

"No, Sergio, wait! You might not be able to get him off!"

He grinned. "Thanks, Parker, but don't worry. Here goes. He's a left-hander, is he?"

I nodded, and Sergio pulled Drog on.

"You traitor!" Drog screamed at me before Sergio had a chance to say anything. "You yellow-bellied mop head!"

Sergio stared at Drog, then at me, then threw his head back and laughed. "Well, he still talks," he said, "and he's friendly as ever."

I bit my lip and tried not to let Drog see how relieved I was.

"You see, Drog?" I said. "Sergio does want you. There was nothing to be afraid of."

"Afraid? *Afraid?* Drog is never afraid."

Blend with him. "Of course not, I forgot. Anyway, they're going to put you in lots of plays—"

"And the first one will be with Jasmine," Sergio said to his Drog hand. "She took a shine to you, my friend."

Drog looked up at Sergio.

"She did, didn't she?"

"Everyone in the troupe will want their chance with you," I said. "You'll be so busy rehearsing and performing and traveling all over the country, you'll hardly have time to sleep."

"And how about you, Boy? Won't you be jealous?"

"I'll try not to be."

"But you have no idea how lost you'll be without me, Parker! Oh well, your problem. You'll just have to come see me when I'm famous."

"I will. Maybe even before."

"Meanwhile, I suppose you're going back to sweating in the doo doo with Sensei?"

"The doo doo?" Sergio said.

"Oh, he means the dojo. Yeah, Drog, that sounds pretty good to me."

"You'd better get your black belt in that peace-fighting if you know what's good for you."

"I'll try, Drog."

"Don't try. Do it!" Drog said.

I laughed. He sounded like Sensei.

I punched Mom's number on my cell phone. "So long, Drog," I said. And then I said something that surprised me. "We've had some good times."

"You're really going? Now? Wait. Did I ever tell you about—"

"No, Drog," I said.

He turned to Sergio. "Well, what are we waiting for? Let's get started with that Jasmine girl." Then he turned back to me. "You still here?"

"C'mon, I'll walk you out," Sergio said.

He slipped Drog right off his hand and laid him on the shelf. A frayed little piece of cloth dropped to the floor, and Sergio picked it up.

"Sergio . . . Drog . . . you just . . . took him off! How?"

He smiled and put his puppet hand around my shoulder. "It gets easier with practice." He handed me the cloth scrap. "Want this for a souvenir?"

It was a label: Made in U.A.E.

Mom drove up and waved, and it hit me. How was I ever going to break it to her about Christmas? Well, first the good news.

I got into the warm car, hiding my left hand in my jacket pocket. Mom waved to Sergio and we watched him walk back to the stage door.

"Well, Parker," she said, "how'd everything go?"

"Surprise!" I pulled out my hand, held it up, and grinned.

"Wha— Parker! He's gone? Really?" She stared at my hand.

So did I. Amazing. It was a little pasty, and there was gunk in all the creases, but otherwise it looked pretty much like the other one.

"Yep. He joined the troupe without me."

"Oh, Darling, this is such wonderful, wonderful news! Congratulations!" Then she yelled "Whoopee!" out the window and headed for the highway. "Wait till your father hears you got rid of that puppet!"

No. "Please, Mom, don't tell Dad or anyone I got *rid* of Drog. Say . . . I got him a job."

I remembered the scrap of a label and pulled it out of my pocket. "Have you ever heard of U.A.E., Mom? I think it's a place."

"Oh, you must mean the United Arab Emirates."

"Emirates? Emir-ates? Is that where emirs come from?"

"Well, it's one of the places, yes."

Ho! So did Drog just make up that boy from Ohio? Did

he really know the emir's son who spoke Gelato? Neither? Both? Did he even know himself anymore? *Drog, you rascal.*

I burst out laughing and couldn't stop. Mom joined in, even though she didn't know what she was laughing about, and each time she caught her breath to say *what?* it just set us both off again. I'd never really thought about the words *belly laugh*, but right then my one-point sure was getting a massage.

Finally we were quiet, and Mom grinned over at me.

Here goes.

"Mom? I want to go visit Dad for Christmas."

The car slowed a bit.

"I see. I guess I'm not surprised."

I waited for her to say something more, but she didn't.

"I know he has trouble being my dad sometimes, but maybe he just needs more practice."

She gazed out the window. "Well he—I believe you're right about that. Parker, I've always thought if only he could just . . . enjoy you. He has no idea what he's missed."

It had begun to snow again. Big soft flakes this time. *Let it last.*

"He's going to take me sledding."

"Ah."

The windshield wipers cleared two fan-shaped windows through the wet whiteness.

"Christmas without you will be awfully lonely, Parker. I'm not going to pretend it won't."

"Yeah I know. Sorry."

She sighed. "And here I was thinking we'd go pick out the tree tomorrow."

"We still can, Mom."

She gave me a half smile. "Of course we can. You're right. We could still have Christmas together, couldn't we? Just a little early."

"Cool!" I said. "Two Christmases!"

She tousled my hair, "You're quite a guy, Parker. You know that?"

I ducked from under her hand.

"Mom? Everything's . . . changing so fast. It's mostly good, I guess, but to tell you the truth, I'm kind of scared."

She swallowed. "I know what you mean," she said. "Me, too."

So we were all scared now—Mom, Dad, and me.

Two Christmases? Could be good. But two families? How would that be? That question mark was getting bigger. *Think about something else, something easier.*

I reached in my pocket for Wren's agate stone and leaned back in the seat, trying to picture myself doing aikido with two free hands. And making things again! I'd have just enough time to carve something for Mom for Christmas. Maybe an ornament for the tree.

Then I remembered I still hadn't told her there wasn't going to be any heat at aikido that night. I didn't tell her.

chapter thirty-five

It was already kind of cool when I got to the dojo. I had just lined my shoes up and stepped barefoot onto the mat when I felt someone rush up behind me.

I spun to the left and caught the wrists of my attacker. *Whooosh! Whooosh!* In seconds we were standing side by side. Laughing. It was Wren.

What a great way to start the long night. She had attacked me as hard as she could. That meant she knew that neither of us would get hurt. She trusted me.

Wren looked down at my left hand, and her eyes got big.

"Parker!" she said. "Where's your friend?"

She lost her concentration for a second, so I pulled down and threw her to the mat. She rolled easily and came up laughing.

I put my hands on her shoulders. "You're my friend," I said.

Expect nothing and be ready for anything, Sensei says. But I wasn't ready when Wren leaned forward on her toes and kissed me, a tiny brush on the cheek.

Suddenly my centered circle turned into a wobbly wheel. All I could do then was fall to the mat and roll.

Wren laughed again and gave me a hand up, and I told her all about Peoria.

"That's great! So you don't have to go to Bradley now, right?"

"No Bradley."

She shut her eyes, and when she opened them again, she wiped one eye with the heel of her hand and smiled.

"Guess what? I found out for sure I'm getting the mouse for Christmas," she said. "A boy mouse. Want to come over after school the day we get out and start working on his house?"

"Can't, Wren," I said, "I'm going to spend Christmas with my dad. And my sister."

"You are? Wow, Parker. That's really something."

"Yeah, it is."

A ripple of little nerves ran under my ribs just thinking about it. Dad would come to get me on Friday and take me to his house for Christmas, and that would be the beginning of—what? *One-point one-point.* We were so different. Could he ever understand me and be happy with me the way I was? I knew he was going to try. But what would I do if he couldn't? I could only be me.

"How about when you get back?" Wren was saying. "I can keep *el ratón* in a cage until then."

"Um . . . el ratón?"

"That's 'mouse' in Spanish. I looked it up."

I laughed. "You would! Sure, let's work on it when I get back. That'll be fun."

I looked down at the hand where Drog used to be and stretched my fingers. It gets easier with practice, Sergio had said. Did that mean he'd been through something like this *lots* of times?

Other students started coming into the dojo.

When Big Boy saw that Drog was gone, he grinned and punched my shoulder. Then the three of us knelt on the mat to wait for Sensei. If it was getting colder in the room, I didn't notice.

I spread both hands out on my knees and relaxed. I could almost hear Drog saying. "You're on your own, Fall Guy! First flame boys, then ninja girls, and now resident rodents! I'm quite sure I have a previous engagement!"

He was right. I was going to miss him, in a way.

THE END

Acknowledgments

Thanks to the many early readers of this story,
both dreamers and sticklers: Lynne Wikoff, Cammy Doi,
Suzanne Kosanke, Marion Coste, Susan Morrison, Ellie
Crowe, Nancy Mower, and Cedric Cowing.

Thanks especially to Tammy Yee for insisting this
must be a novel, to Donna Jo Napoli for pointing out how
scary it could be if..., to Eric McCutcheon for sharing
valuable insights long-distance, and to Jim Rumford for
pondering the words and fates of characters with me in
kitchen-table sessions.

Thanks to all-night readers Scott Goto and Vicky
Dworkin, and to Elizabeth Oh, possibly Drog's biggest fan.

Thanks to fairy godmother Sarah Davies of
Greenhouse Literary for loving Drog and Parker at first
sight; for her unfailing cheer, support, and savvy; and for
her questions that continually raised the stakes.

Last but not least, thanks to my editor Andrew Karre
for knowing right away he wanted to do this book and for
his inspiring questions, ideas, and know-how.

Have I forgotten someone? Oh, yes. The truth is, I owe
everything to Drog.